I0621541

BARE ALLEY INK: VOLUME ONE

EVERNIGHT PUBLISHING ®

www.evernightpublishing.com

BARE ALLEY INK: VOLUME ONE

DEDICATION

To the late great Doris O'Connor who loved this idea. To Karyn for her invaluable input and everyone at Evernight Publishing for all they do to get the book from me to you, the reader.

To everyone who reads and enjoys my books, thank you

BARE ALLEY INK: VOLUME ONE

THE TATTOO ARTIST'S MATE

Bare Alley Ink, 1

Doris O'Connor and Raven McAllan

Copyright © 2019

Prologue

"I have decided, pet, it is selfish of me to keep you to myself." Julian smiled at Isla in a way that made her skin crawl. What did he mean? Dare she ask? She opened her mouth, but he forestalled her in a simple effective manner. He put his hand over hers, his little finger curled inside her lips. She smelled, and tasted, snuff. Taking snuff was a horrible, archaic, disgusting habit Julian had cultivated. It made her want to sneeze and throw up in equal measures.

"Now, pet, be careful. You know what happens when my pet gets above herself. Remember I know what's best."

Did he? Lately Isla had begun to doubt that. Surely his "I know best, do as I say attitude" could be tempered at times? Weren't subs supposed to be able to say "enough"? Why did he know best? And why for fuck's sake did he call her pet? Oh, she knew a lot of Doms used the affectionate sobriquet, but from Julian it sounded false. As if he had decided he needed to sound Dom-like and thought that was the way. She could have told him it didn't. If she dared.

Good lord, what had she become? Shame flooded her. She was a mouse. A pathetic, groveling, couldn't stand up for herself mouse.

"Isla, are you listening?"

Argh, she'd tuned out. Not very sub like. Maybe she wasn't sub material after all? "Sorry."

The tap to her cunt was short, sharp, and hurt. "Listen now. I've said I'm not going to keep you to myself. I will share you with my friends,"

You what?

Had she heard that right? "Say that again." In her shock she forgot the "Sir".

His eyes narrowed. "Don't be disrespectful. Whoever I decide can have you. However I decide. You heard and earned a punishment. I'll let Harry Thurston give it. You are for all of us."

Harry Thurston? He was renowned as a sadist.

"No."

Julian appeared flabbergasted. She was a bit gobsmacked herself. Where had that come from?

"What do you mean no?" He snarled the words.

"No, I won't."

"You will or—"

"No and no or nothing. It's over." Isla heard herself and wanted to high five. It was. "No more, I've had enough. I quit."

His eyes narrowed. "You go, and it's forever, pet. How will you cope, eh? No Sir to protect you, show you where you are going wrong. You'll soon come crawling back."

She grinned, confident now that he was not what she needed.

"I'll manage very well."

"With that reminder of who you belong to?" He pointed at her ankle where he'd insisted she have his name tattooed.

Isla trembled but managed a creditable, scornful laugh. "That? I'll get it lasered off." She grabbed her handbag, turned on her heel and marched out. Out of his house and out of his life.

Chapter One

Six months later

Isla woke up in a sweat. That bloody dream again. Why bears for goodness' sake? Oh, she liked her shifter stories—who didn't? There was nothing nicer that a hot bloke with a body like a Greek god who in the blink of an eye changed from said bloke to a—well in her case it seemed a bear—to make a girl wet and wanting. Most times a session with her bullet usually helped. Not now though. For some reason she woke up sated and strange though it seemed, with a feeling she wasn't herself. That someone or something had changed her. Almost, she thought, as if she'd had some sort of out of body experience.

Which of course was daft. She was no shifter. Her mum was from Auchtermuchty in Scotland and her dad an out and out cockney, who he said was related to Pearly Kings and Queens. Not that she believed that bit. Her granddad had been a coalman and her grandma allegedly a bit weird. A lady who Isla remembered as small and white haired, who smelled of cough drops and told the most amazing stories about wizards and dragons.

Maybe that was it? She was subconsciously remembering those stories. Wasn't one about a bear who was lonely and wanted a mate? And found a human instead?

Wouldn't that be good? Isla sniggered and rolled her eyes.

"Too much cheese."

Was that really a growl she heard, or the bin lorry doing its usual gear-crunching reverse around the corner? She poked her head between the curtains. The lane outside the house was empty. Not even her next-door neighbor going for his usual early morning jog with Pongo his sheepdog.

Nothing except the trees across the lane waving as if someone—or something—had recently rushed through them.

"For us, I'm watching over you."

Isla shivered. Where had that stupid thought come from? She headed for the shower and remembered her vow.

Today is the day.

****

"Bare Alley, third on left." Isla muttered to herself as she parked her car in the multi-story of her nearest town, got out and locked up. "Stupid name for a street." Okay it was probably steeped in the deep dark annals of time and full of mystery and intrigue, but it still didn't seem right. It reminded her of naked orgies, Lady Godiva, and a picture she'd seen in an art gallery of a bear with a naked lady. Both looked happy. It made her miserable. Where had *her* happy gone? Her joie de vivre? Her love of life and all things ridiculous?

Down the toilet.

It was galling to admit that those bloody months with Julian had eroded them. As he'd tried to mold her into his … his what? Not a sub for sure, his slave in a most unpleasant way perhaps? She understood that now. He was, to put no finer point on it, a charlatan. Isla could hit herself for being so taken in. But the man was a smooth talking, persuasive, slimy toad. And Isla realized she had been ripe for someone to love. At university, all her mates had paired off, and nerdy Isla Cameron hadn't. She'd been more concerned with good grades and aiming for a career in something esoteric.

Instead she'd fallen into his lap and life, forgotten esoteric, spent a miserable few months before she jumped out of said lap and then indulged in her love of cakes. Which added several inches to her already ample hips as of course at first, she couldn't make, bake and sell such things without sampling them. Now she was more sensible, but those inches clung to her like an insecure child who didn't want to leave its mum. However, she was happy within herself, and if having to buy new trousers was a result of that happiness so be it.

Being you own boss was great up to a point. But when you were so successful you had to ask a mate if you could switch your answering machine to her phone so you could have a day off as well as your normal Monday and Tuesday, it wasn't on. Not really.

Oh, she enjoyed Isla's Bakes, was happy to do bespoke celebration cakes for whoever wanted one, and enjoyed the success she'd achieved. However, it had taken off so well, she needed help. Help she hadn't so far discovered. Her one employee was perfect, but oh how one or two more part-timers would give them more normal working hours not the ten- and twelve-hour days she seemed to be putting in more and more.

She yearned for time to breath and relax and think. Not just about work. About her other current dilemma as well.

As in, her bloody, fucking stupid, tattoo.

Needs must.

Isla had dithered for months over where to go and how get rid of that blasted stupid and she hadn't even wanted it, tattoo, that Julian had insisted on. At first, she was more concerned about sorting her life out than being de-inked or whatever you called it.

Thank God she'd never moved in with Julian. Even when he'd tried to pull the "I'm your Dom, you will live with me" stunt. He'd about begged, but she'd stayed firm, thank heaven. Then he'd suggested he moved in with her instead. Lucky for her, Isla had a ready-made excuse, even though she wasn't sure why she needed it. It was her mum's house, not hers. And she was only house sitting on the understanding there were no extra inhabitants.

That was a lie. Her mum was the most open-minded person she knew, but it was a good get out. Whatever it was that warned her to take things slowly she had no idea, but boy did she give thanks for it.

"I told you, I watch over my own."

That damned voice in her head again. And a growl? Isla glanced around. The alley was almost deserted. A black cat slunk across from one doorway to another. Too far away for her to hear a noise from it. Two schoolboys jostled each other as they came out of the chippy, a poke of chips and a can of something fizzy in their hands. No one else around. She must stop eating too much before bed. Maybe she needed to switch from coffee to water?

It was next step time. As in ditch the crappy tattoo, not switch to water. Isla had researched laser removal but wondered if it might be better just to change it somehow. There was pain, and yeah, there was pain. If she'd discovered one thing from Slimy Julian, it was she really didn't *do* pain. Plus, as there was no guarantee a laser removal would take it all away, maybe a wee change might be better. It was enough of an incentive for her to at least ask. After all, Julian wasn't a lot to hide as roses, a wallflower or a snake or something? She was partial to wallflowers and got the heebie-jeebies over snakes. Maybe not a snake then. Something pleasant. Trailing ivy? Hearts and flowers? Glencoe? Nope that might be a bit too controversial. Whatever, she'd suffer that amount of pain it gave her for a good cause.

After a long while, cussing, moaning, vowing to

cut the said Julian's balls off—that was once she'd read up on a D/s relationship and realized that was what they hadn't had—Isla was ready to say fuck him, forget him, and properly move on.

Hence this first peek at "Bear at the Bare".

What a stupid name for a tattoo parlor. After all, why Bare? For that matter, why Bear? Okay she'd seen a picture of the bloke who ran it, and yeah, he was big, hairy, and she could see him as a grizzly, but please. Why so fucking twee? Did he make sure all his tattoos had bare-naked ladies peeking out from some shrubbery? If so, he could go fly. She didn't want ladies bare or otherwise on her skin. Or men. She wasn't an exhibitionist.

Isla hesitated and took a deep breath. *Pull up your big girl panties time.* It was the one place recommended the most. Lots of five-star reviews. Not just for, as one customer put it, "the hot as hell if he played his cards right, he could have me" tattoo artist, but because he did a superb job. Artist, it was proclaimed, was an understatement. The photos on his web seemed to confirm that.

If only he wasn't a MacDonald. Her granny would have a fit about her "puir wee bairn" putting her body in the hands of a MacDonald in any which way. Granny Campbell still hadn't forgotten or forgiven the so-called treachery of the Clan MacDonald at Glencoe. The fact that the battle—or massacre depending on which side you supported—was over 400 years earlier didn't sway her. Granny Campbell was a staunch supporter of her clan and its history, and had done her best to make Isla understand why.

For Isla it was all a long while ago, and if that was bad of her so be it. One of her best mates at school had been a Campbell. So what? Isla was more concerned with getting the best re-tattoo possible than centuries-old grudges. After all, was he going to come at her with a broadsword or a musket?

As long as he wasn't one of the old guard, it wasn't likely. Maybe he'd refuse to touch her.

She heard that damned growl again.

Chapter Two

Gaspar MacDonald wiped over the addition to his clan mate's ever-growing sleeve, and applied the moisturizer with a smirk.

"You know the rules now."

Josh nodded. "Ad nauseam. I won't do anything daft like showering and so on. Looks good, eh?" He held his arm out to inspect it in the mirror.

"Well, duh, look who did it?" Gaspar smirked. "Only the best will do."

Josh rolled his eyes. "Always one to hide your excellence under a bush, eh? Ever the understatement."

Gaspar laughed. "I tell it like it is. You gonna run out of room on here soon, bro. Best hope this one is a lad, eh."

The fifth bear cub ran away merrily with its siblings in an intertwined dance that made Gaspar's chest feel tight. He'd had the privilege of designing this sleeve from the beginning, when Josh had first encountered his mate. The man had staggered into the studio as soon as it opened, begged for coffee and anything, *anything* to eat and told Gaspar he'd met his life partner. He confessed they'd spent all night sitting on the beach—no sex, just cuddling to keep warm—and waited to watch the sun come up before setting home.

In a whirlwind romance even for shifters, he'd wedded and bedded and got her with five adorable cubs in the space of six years. What's more, the two were still as besotted with each other as the day they'd first clapped eyes on each other. Mates, husband and wife and Dom and sub. Something that Gaspar was beginning to realize he craved for himself. Anyone would think he was turning forty soon, instead of thirty-five, but hooking up with random women when the need struck him to scratch that itch had long lost its appeal. He was ready, more than ready, for permanence. If only he could find the fucking time to go searching for "the one". Dreams were all well and good, but no substitute fro the real thing. Okay, he woke up wet and wanting, and knew enough that they meant something—the shadowy woman in them was going to be important to him, but not how and when. He needed to know her *now*. Before his bloody cock shriveled up from underuse. If only she'd just appear and show him who she was, and let him get laid and sated.

He was so busy, he barely had time for toilet breaks, let alone take a day off to go mate hunting. And if he did, where the fuck would he start? Shifter mating wasn't a website easily found.

Josh grinned and punched Gaspar playfully into the shoulder. Gaspar rolled with it and bared his teeth at the younger guy, while swallowing a growl. They were on their own in the shop so he could let his grizzly show a little, but fuck only knew why his inner beast was so volatile today. It's as though his bear was expecting something momentous to happen. Yeah, he was getting maudlin in his old age.

Happenings didn't happen for him.

"You know darn well, I dinnae give two hoots about whether this one is another girl," Josh stated. "Besides you know my Bella. Balls of steel, and the girls take after her. Wee Aimee is already shifting, and she's not in her teens yet. Just five and growling like an adult. Precocious or what? Still, we'll see what we've been given and love him or her for who they are."

Fantastic sentiments and ones that Gaspar hoped he got the chance to emulate one day. "You can't do better than your Bella." He mimed a kiss. "If she had a sister I'd be at the front of the queue."

"No sister and she's mine, all mine." Josh roared with laughter as Gaspar mock-scowled. "Go get yourself someone like her and ye'll be in clover.'

Gaspar rolled his eyes. "One of a kind." He stood up and stretched to get the kinks out of his body. The aching sort of kinks, sadly. *Fuck and bugger.* When was the last time he'd let his Dom persona out and take over? So fucking long he couldn't remember.

Josh walked to the till and took his wallet out. "What's the dama—holy shit."

The door to the shop blew open with a bang that rattled the windows nearby as a sudden gust of wind blew through the aperture and lifted a sheaf of drawings from the desk. They fluttered around like overlarge confetti and landed in a haphazard heap on the floor.

"Dammit, I should have shut that back door earlier," Gaspar said with a growl that would put the fear of God into anyone who wasn't on his side. "Sodding through draft. The back alley's like a wind tunnel today. You could test a jumbo jet in there and—what the fuck."

Gaspar couldn't have stopped the animalistic growl that rumbled out from his chest if his life depended on it, and he wasn't sure he hadn't grown a few inches, too, because the scent on that breeze....

It couldn't be, yet his bear responded to the call in the wind with another deep, menacing growl, which shook the floorboards and made the bell above his shop door go into spasms.

It was her. It had to be. The woman he'd been with in her sleep. Oh, he hadn't seen her face, wasn't told her name, just that when he met her, he would know. And he did. That hair... Her. *Mine.* The woman he yearned for, had wet dreams about, and knew was his. She'd come to him.

The gorgeous, fuckable, female human with carroty hair and big, expressive eyes who stood in the doorway jumped, took a step back, and bit her lip. As he watched, she squared her shoulders and stared at him. Was he the only one who saw the effort it cost her? How could Josh be unaware? Or was he being tactful?

Josh whistled through his teeth and laid a wad of cash on the counter, as he looked between Gaspar and the young woman now standing hesitantly in the doorway.

"Right, okay well, I say, I'll best be off then. Er, take care and thanks. I'll let you know if we need another one. See you around, Gaspar. Miss. Here ye go. He doesnae bite…" He held the door open for the redhead who seemed to be as mesmerized with Gaspar as his bear and him were in her, and ushered her in. "Well not unless he's provoked or…"

Not tactful then. Bastard.

"Josh, zip it."

Josh laughed. "Aye, right oh. He's okay miss, honestly. An awkward bugger, but a fine one. You've nowt to fear from him." He turned back to Gaspar, winked and mouthed "good luck". Gaspar was certain the sod said something along the lines of "he'll fuck you senseless given half a chance".

Which was true, but only with her consent and her knowledge of what it would mean. His bear was very much aware of her and if they mated—not just screwed or fucked, but made love—she'd have no chance to leave without one hell of a dust up. Mated meant for life and that was that.

Whatever she was.

Gaspar ignored Josh, the fucker, and sniffed the air again. Human? Seemed like it.

His heat sank. That made life twice as hard.

"I'm away." Josh raised his hand in farewell, and

Gaspar grunted. No doubt Josh would tell Bella all about the carrot-top with the big eyes and gorgeous figure, and Bella would come around demanding the gen, but that was for later. Now every fiber of his being was focused on the redhead. Who looked as if she didn't know whether to throw up or do a runner.

Josh meanwhile laid one large hand on the girl's shoulder. "Do come in, lassie. I know he looks mean, but he's the best. We're friends from way back, and there's no one I'd trust more to ink me." He waved his inked sleeve at her. "You're in good hands."

Gaspar flipped Josh the finger, which elicited a cock-hardening gasp from the woman staring at him. Wide, deep, moss-colored eyes a man could drown in, full lips, which simply invited him to taste, to devour. Curves in all the right places and breasts... He nigh on salivated. Breasts to fill his hands and more. Breasts to suckle, nip, and lave.

He let his gaze move higher and was mesmerized. He couldn't tear his gaze away from her slender throat at the base of which a pulse beat a rapid staccato in tune to his, and his bear grumbled anew.

Know it, take hold of it. Mine. His. *Fuck a duck.* As he thought, he was committed to a human? *Mine, all mine, and sod the human bit. I'll sort it somehow. She is the woman I've dreamed about.*

As thought processes went these were as caveman-like as they came. Bloody alien to him as well. What the fuck? However, there again, it wasn't every day that the one woman destined to be with you walked in your shop like an offering from the gods above. She might not know it, but he as sure as hell did. She *was* his mate. From then on and forever. All he had to do was show her, persuade her and... His brain didn't process anything beyond that.

His mate's eyes widened further, and she took an involuntary step—toward him, he noticed, not away—which had no doubt been her intention, if the confused look in her expressive eyes was any indication. A trembling hand pushed her long mane of riotous red curls away from her face, and now Gaspar had the devil of a job to keep his eyes off the impressive cleavage straining against the sensible blouse she wore tucked into her jeans. There wasn't an ounce of artifice about his mate, not a speck of make-up on her face. Just vibrant, delicious woman, with lush curves to die for and the sweetest scent, which made his bear damn near itch to burst through his skin. To claim, to devour, to mark.

Mine.

He did neither, of course. That would send her screaming. Now. So he simply inhaled deeply, satisfied to not scent any specific attachment to another male. Not that it would have mattered to his bear. His beast was all but ready to tear the throat out of any man, or animal, who dared brush up against his mate, and make no mistake about it, this woman would be his. She just didn't know it yet.

Boy was she in for a surprise. Hell, he hoped it would be a good one.

Mindful of the fact that he must look like a complete asshole, Gaspar forced a smile on his face, scrubbed his hand over his beard and somehow got his vocal cords to work.

"Sorry about Josh." He waved towards the alley where Josh had by then disappeared. "He means well, but his sense of humor needs working on, big time. Sometimes as his wife says, he's not too big for a skelp around the lug and needs it. Anyway, enough of him. Come on in. What can I do for you today?" Gaspar did his best to keep the possessive note out of his voice. He wasn't sure he managed it, but what the fuck? It couldn't be helped, and it was certain it would just get stronger as time went on. She might as well get used to it now rather than later.

Baby steps. Fuck it, I'll just try to do steps, and not tell her everything at once. It wasn't going to be easy to explain himself to an unsuspecting human. Baby steps might be best. If only he knew what the hell they were. Why in all the world had a human been sent for him?

"Take your time." He handed her a bottle of water. She took it, unscrewed the cap, and took a long, slow swig before she recapped the bottle.

"I, well that is, I'm not sure you can, it's just..." Heat rose in her cheeks under his silent scrutiny, and the wave of protectiveness that engulfed Gaspar made his chest feel tight. When had he ever experienced such an emotion before?

Like, never. It was unnerving to say the least.

He crossed the distance between them in a few long strides, and she jumped when he placed his large hand over hers to gently pry away the death grip she still had on the door.

"Come in and sit down." He did his best to keep his animal under control and not let it bleed into his body, or his voice. Soft and unthreatening was needed, not macho and bear. "Whatever it is, it's got something to do with a tattoo, I bet, and I can most definitely help with that." He smiled down on her, and some of her underlying tension went out of her small frame.

"It's my forte," he added. "I can do what you need."

So small, and delicate, she fit right under his armpit. No doubt she didn't see herself like that, but for him, she was perfect. To have and to hold.

Down, boy, don't frighten her.

"Is this where you're saying 'trust me, I'm a tattoo artist'?" Her voice, while still wobbly, held a certain amount of snark, and Gaspar grinned.

"That what the one said who gave you whatever you want changed?" he countered, and she narrowed her eyes, put her hand on her hips and stepped into the shop at last. The door banged shut, and she jumped a little in surprise.

"How do you know that's what happened? I might just fancy getting my first one." She raised her gaze to his briefly and promptly dropped it to his collarbone when he raised an eyebrow in silent query.

"Then I would stand corrected, but that's not the case this time, is it?" he said gently. There was no point in anything confrontational. "And how I know? Let's just say, I've been in the business a long time, and I'm very good at reading people. So, where is it? Why do you want it removed? What's your name, and how do you take your coffee?"

He winked at her sharp inhale, and she relaxed further and sat down on the plush settee he kept for waiting customers. A sod to remember not to let any shifter near when aroused—he'd lost four already to sharp claws and teeth—but perfect for ambience. His little human darted a glance toward the book of sketches and photos of past tattoos and then looked up at him.

"On my ankle. 'Cause it's the dumb name of my ex. Isla Campbell, and white coffee, no sugar, please."

"Sweet enough already?" he asked with a smirk, and she rolled her eyes.

"How original and nope, I'm told I'm rather tart, but sugar goes straight to my hips if I as much as look at it."

Gaspar led his gaze linger on said parts of her, and her breathing sped up under his silent perusal, which pleased the possessive animal in him no end. Already her scent was beginning to take on a personal note, one which any other shifter would understand to mean that she was spoken for. That she had a mate whether she knew it or not.

In this case probably not.

"And damn fine hips they are, too, if you ask me." He smiled at her as he handed her a cup of the steaming brew and then sat next to her. The sofa dipped under his considerable bulk, which, as he well knew, meant she slid toward him with a little squeak. Their thighs touched, and even through the layers of denim separating them, the connection between them arched, shimmering in almost visible tremors. Gaspar wanted nothing more than to wrap his arms around her and to tell her it was okay. That she was safe. That no one would ever hurt her again, but he had to tread easy. To spook her away now, to let on how much he knew about her just from that accidental touch, how much his bear was itching to hunt down the fucker whose name she wore on her ankle, was not his intention.

The beast would get his revenge in due course. For now, he sat back, smiled and nodded.

"Okay, so tell me the story, and we'll come up with a plan."

"Well…"

Five minutes later her litany of her tattoo finished. "So I walked, and now need to get rid of that last reminder of my stupidity."

"We're all stupid at times," Gaspar said in his deep, growly voice. "But I know just the thing to get rid of yours. How do you fancy a bear and a honeypot instead?"

Chapter Three

Bear? Honeypot?

Why was her skin clammy, hot and cold all at once? Why were her nipples hard and sore, and why did she want to jump his bones? That was *so* not her. What the hell was going on? Had the tattoo guy hypnotized her? Why was he staring at her so intently? And why, for fuck's sake did his eyes glow? Why so many whys?

Questions bombarded her, and she swallowed hard to make sure her nausea didn't overwhelm her. She was *not* going to throw up.

"Baby?"

That dragged her attention back to him big time.

Baby? Oh no not a baby, never ever, nada, niet, nein, and bloody no. "Excuse me?" The frost in her voice made her wince. It didn't seem to much please the big, hunky tattoo artist either. Tough, except … those glowing eyes flashed, and she could swear he growled.

Growled? Not just a deep baritone with gravelly undertones but a proper growl. Good grief, those late-night shifter movies were much too graphic and she watched way too many if that were the direction in which her mind headed.

Enough already.

"Baby?"

Sheesh that voice, impatient or not, made her pussy clench and her clit throb.

Automatic climax. Except.

No, not in a million years. Asshole. Isla let her temper free. Hadn't she decided she was no longer a doormat? Well, nor was she anybody's baby. Except her mum and dad's and even they'd passed the stage of calling her that many years earlier.

"I, *mate,* am nobody's baby." She poked him in the chest, amazed at her temerity.

He narrowed his eyes and raised one eyebrow.

"I haven't been for the last twenty-seven or so years," Isla said firmly. Or she hoped she did. She wasn't too sure there hadn't been a wee tremor in her voice. "No goo, goo, ga, ga, fart, giggle, shit and pee over anyone. I can walk, talk, go to the loo unaided and hit the porcelain without wetting the floor. Oh, and guess what? I can add up my checkbook, well I would if we still had the darned things, am articulate and intelligent and able to stand up for myself." *Okay maybe that should be I am trying bloody damned hard.* "Not a baby, get it? My name is Isla. Or Miss Campbell to you."

To her relief his expression changed from thunderous to amused, and he chuckled as he shook his head.

"Feisty, eh? I see interesting times ahead."

There was that damned glow in his eyes again. It made her want to fidget and look anywhere but at his face. The trouble was if she lowered her gaze not only did it bring an impressive bulge in his jeans to eye level, it reminded her of things she wanted to forget. Not the bulge but the lowered eyes stuff.

Bloody Julian. Is he going to ruin the rest of my life as well? To her utmost relief Isla got her mad back in spades. *Sod it, I am not a coward.* Isla stared at the tattoo guy and dared him to comment on her expression.

"Mate, that's for sure. Campbell? That's too bad." He flicked her chin up. "But I'll cut you a break. You can't help your ancestors. No, don't bristle, it's true. As for the rest? No more poking. It irritates me. And, listen well, I'm not into scat or golden showers so you've nothing to worry about there. I want you in a much more sensual way."

Scat? Gold... Heat rushed into her cheeks. What was he? She pulled herself up to her full five feet three. No mean feat when she was sitting, or more to the point, slumping, on a big squishy sofa with a hunk of a man so close she could feel his body heat, and sense his own personal scent. Arousing was an understatement. Why she had no idea. Sweaty men didn't usually do anything for her. Now though?

Hold on. Was there a damp animal about? She could swear she could smell one. Maybe not politic to ask. She chose to reply to his last words instead.

"That is not the sort of thing I want to talk about." Shit, what did she sound like? Talk about up herself. "It's..." What was it? "Nothing to do with me."

He did that bloody sniff thing again, nodded and smirked. "Fair enough if you think so. Up to me to show you different. Later. Now, shall we talk about everything else?"

"What?" There was nothing else, surely? Except how soon could she get off the sofa and be out of there. Tattoo be damned. There must be somewhere else she could clear off. This was all a bit much. "Nothing to talk about. I better go."

He shook his head, and his hair flew around him like a tawny halo. "You better not. There's plenty to talk about. Like why you're here. Apart from changing a tattoo."

"That's all I'm here for."

He grinned, and she blinked as he tapped her nose. A couple of his pearly whites didn't seem innocent. More like...

Fangs? Oh, shut up now, Isla. Enough of the animal stuff. But the tap on the nose was like a tattoo in itself. A tap of possession. That wasn't on.

"Do not touch me, you, you...." She stopped

speaking as his eyes narrowed and his lips firmed. "I don't like it or want it."

"Tut-tut. Don't lie, sweet Isla, or you'll see punishment before pleasure and that's a promise. We both know there's more to it than that."

It *was* definitely time she went. Punishment? In his dreams. She fingered the sock full of sand in her pocket. It would make a great cosh if need be, and had been recommended to her by her mum as a precaution. Mum meant in case Julian appeared, but Isla thought it just sensible for any scenario.

Never mind the tattoo change, if there were no other shops she thought acceptable, she'd live with it and wear socks or wellies.

Isla grabbed hold of her handbag and maneuvered herself off the sofa and onto her feet. Boy she bet she looked about as elegant as an elephant doing the tango. Did elephants dance? Maybe she meant a chimpanzee or … a bear or … *godallmightystop it.* The man's nearness was sending her crazy. She gave herself a stern talking to and him a frosty smile. The one that most men, when they saw it, took a step back, babbled some sort of apology or whatever, and got the hell out of Dodge.

Not Gaspar MacDonald. Oh no, he, the bugger, gave a very unusual grin, stood up in one fluid movement she envied and took a step forward. Typical nose in MacDonald. She was the one who moved away.

Forward, back, it's like a bloody dance. Next, we'll be do-si-do-ing or bowing before we do a two-step. Bring back today, please. Enough already. If she hadn't been so unsettled it could have been amusing.

"Don't come near me." Lordy, was that shrill squeak really her? It was pathetic. Isla cleared her throat. "If you do, I'll have to take drastic measures," she said firmly, pleased her voice didn't break, she didn't stutter and actually did sound as if she meant what she said. "Scream, kick, sue or something."

"Definitely scream or something, baby," he said in an amused, gravelly voice that did strange things to her insides and *oh fuck* made her panties damp.

"That's my promise and my oath," he finished and pinched her cheek.

God, who the hell did he think he was? "You know what? You're screwy. Baby for fuck's sake." She shook her head. "Why not be really original? Honey boo, sweetie, sugar lump, pussycat, booty cakes... Argh. No, never, ever. It's all touched in the head weird. Why the hell did anyone think this was the place to get a tattoo altered? I'll use a permanent marker instead." She headed for the door and pushed it open. "Sorry I've changed my mind."

He smirked. "I thought you said you'd wear socks."

Isla blinked as the door slammed shut and just missed her toes. She knew she hadn't spoken that sentiment out loud. Ever since bloody Julian she'd been very careful about what she said and what she thought. That had been a *thought*.

"Why do you say that?' She almost added "asshole", but the expression on his face stopped her. He looked ... like a proper Dom. "Si..." *Oops, no, not Sir. Not ever again.* "Seems daft to me," she added hastily. "Socks indeed."

"Ah, sweet Isla, you are so heading for a fall if you insist on lying to me." He pinched her cheek, then pressed his lips to the spot.

Never mind tattoo, that touch seared her like nothing ever had. Talk about spooky.

"Pet, just try to trust me, eh? Take me as one who has your best interests at heart. To me, my pet means the one I care for most, the one who means most to me. My soul mate, my life. If it suits," he lowered his voice to a sexy murmur. "My sub. What else would you say?"

All the names she'd read in her hot as hades stories filled her mind. So did the way reading them made her hot, wet, wanting, and bloody horny. The damp panties became wet, and goosebumps covered her body. So why was she thinking *"no, not in a million years, proper, improper, impromptu or imposter, not gonna happen."*

Sodding Julian of course. How would she know what a proper Dom looked like any way? She'd thought she'd found one in Julian, and that was a big fat, not on your Nellie, damp squid if there ever was one. Great judge of character she obviously wasn't. So what if this guy made her panties wet, her juices gather and her nipples so hard it was a wonder they hadn't put holes in her blouse? So what if he tugged on every sense she possessed? So what if he made her want to renege on her vow of no more men? *So what?* How did she judge what was real and what was wishful thinking?

"I know more about you than you imagine, sweet Isla. Do you want to listen? Or." He lowered his voice. "Are you gonna chicken out?"

"Cluck, de cluck."

Gaspar chuckled. "Oh pet, we're going to have so much fun."

She shuddered. "Not pet. Please not pet."

"Baby? Ma Belle?"

She sighed. "Baby makes me want to puke. Ma Belle? Unoriginal but if you have to. Pet reminds me of something nasty I'd rather forget."

He scrutinized her for a long minute, until she was ready to squirm and then gave one decisive nod. "So wouldn't it be better to give you happy, not nasty associations with it…" He paused and then said emphatically. "Pet."

Isla thought about it for a second or two. What he said made sense but… "With the proviso if it icks me out you stop and swap?"

"I promise."

"Then I'll do my best not to baa, bark, or meow."

He snorted.

"Now, pet. Behave. Let's have fun. Oh, and I promise I can make you purr, pet."

Okay, it wasn't the time to decide what he meant by fun. Or why her heart was still missing the odd beat and she felt lightheaded. Now was "do I, don't I, get this tattoo changed"? For a start anyway. Isla accepted her life was about to change, and for once she was sure it would be for the better.

However, why was he staring at her so intently? And sniffing at her for God's sake. She couldn't smell. She hadn't eaten garlic, had enjoyed a shower, and used her favorite body spray, and it was no way was it warm enough to negate that. He was just plain rude.

"Do you need a hanky?" She fished a tissue from her pocket and held it out. "Here. It's clean."

"What?" He glanced at it and then away again to stare at her face.

Did she have a dirty mark on her cheek? A spot on her nose? She was sure she didn't. But his eyes bored into her, like a laser or a heat-seeking missile with the emphasis on heat. Isla surreptitiously wafted the hem of her blouse around.

"You're sniffing. I hate sniffers. Blow your nose."

Gaspar made a noise somewhere between a snort and a howl. *Did you call it a snowl?* Whatever it was, it was unusual and very, very, hot. Her juices began to make a slow slide down her legs, and Isla pushed her thighs together. That was all she needed. Not.

"Woman, you're off the plot."

Chapter Four

Gaspar couldn't remember the last time he'd had so much fun. He couldn't help but tease. The memory of how her thoughts had invaded his had popped out without him thinking amazed and delighted him. His woman—for whatever she thought, his sweet pet *was* his—was a walking mass of delicious cock-hardening contradictions. Of course she didn't know he could hear her thoughts as clear as his own if he chose to, but oh, how he'd like to threaten to wash her mouth out for her little and not so little white lies. Not that he would, that sort of thing wasn't in his repertoire, but a nice wee scribe with his claw would make her stop and think. And show anyone who needed to that she was his. Plus of course, he'd willingly demonstrate to her how to mark him as hers. Gaspar was all for equality in that respect. Then one day, show her what they could be if she accepted and...

Ha, in his dreams. She would more than likely laugh and tell him to get out of fancy dress than accept that part of him.

For now. However, he'd worry about that later. Now, he just wanted her to accept she was his. He made himself turn off his ability to tune in to her. It wasn't right, or ethical, to eavesdrop one someone's thoughts unless absolutely necessary. Especially now he knew who she was. Last time he'd not been prepared. It was part of their creed that you only heard the thoughts of those who mattered, who were part of you. In theory.

In practice? Faint hope.

His woman stuck her nose in the air. "I do not appreciate you speaking to me that way." Her words were defiant, her demeanor, anything but. "What planet are you on. Owww, you bully."

He'd given in to the temptation to growl, swing her around and tap her ass. Not too hard, but with enough force to sting.

Isla glared. "Do you like your body the way it is? Or do you want your balls rearranged?" She bit her lip and blushed. "Sod it. I mean—oh God, you make me so cross, and I never lose my temper. I came in to talk about a tattoo and ended up being molested. And don't you bloody growl at me. What do you think you are? An animal?"

What would she say if he said "yes"?

"Some say so," Gaspar said equably. "You'll make your own mind up when you're ready."

"Argh." Isla threw her hands up in the air. "How the hell did we get to this?"

"Fate."

"Fate?" she asked incredulously. "Don't talk rot."

"You'll learn. We are fated to be what we are to each other." He didn't think it was the time to go into details. Or tell her what he'd heard from her and what he'd seen.

"Oh, all right then," she said, deadpan. "Fate. Yeah. Why does it hate me? Tell it to give me a break already."

Gaspar watched as all the temper drained out of her. She looked … forlorn he decided. Lonely, unhappy, and bewildered. A horrible state to be in. Would she let him help her?

"I always said I didn't believe in fate," Isla said flatly. "No point."

"Serendipity?" he suggested. "Like knows like? A meeting of minds? True love finds a way? One of those things?"

She snorted. "You're off your trolley. I've got to

go." She tugged her hand from his, where he'd held her to him. "Please."

"Okay, no more." *Yet.* "Let's start again," Gaspar said. He couldn't let her walk away in the state she was in. Okay, he couldn't let her walk away, period. "Hello, I'm Gaspar MacDonald. Owner and inker, Bear at the Bare. How can I help you, Miss…"

He held his breath.

****

Isla considered the man who stood next to her. Much to her amazement, he'd intrigued her, interested her, aroused her, and yeah, as her mate would say, "hornified" her. Horny was an understatement. If she took off her panties—and she didn't intend to—she'd be able to wring them out. Her nipples ached, her clit throbbed, and she needed to get out of there and find her bullet pretty damned quick.

"I'm Isla Campbell. I, er, well look, this is a bit embarrassing," she said in a rush. "I've been an idiot and agreed to get my asshole of an ex's name tattooed on my ankle. And now I need it gone." She stopped for a moment and thought over what she'd said. "Scrub part of that, I don't think I did really agree. Asshole Julian told me as his sub I had to, and I … rrghh…" She took a stumbling step back as Gaspar's eyes became more amber than ever and flashed with rage. She could swear his hands curled into claws, and his features began to change. He reminded her of an unfriendly grizzly about to pounce. What next?

She grabbed hold of the wall as the floor shook.

"I'm sorry," she gasped. "But you're scaring me and…" *Holy hell, was that a growl? I really do have bears on the brain.* "Gaspar, Mr. MacDonald, whoever, whatever, please, stop it."

"He was no dom." Gaspar shook his head and

took a deep breath. "Sorry I scared you. Give me a minute. I was angry."

How weird she could tell he didn't invest the word Dom with a capital D.

"I guessed that," Isla said dryly. "Later. When I realized he wasn't I got out pretty damned quick. But damage was done. Oh, not physically," she added in a hurry as Gaspar's eyes flashed again. "But it took me a while before I cottoned on to the fact he was a fraud. A charlatan." Her voice shook as once again she thought how stupid she'd been. "A wannabe with nothing going for him. God, I was so clueless." She thumped the chair arm, wishing it was bloody Julian. "I'm happy now to be me, and me I'll stay. A happier me if you can get his bloody name off my ankle. I'll go with a honeypot."

Gaspar nodded. "And a bear. You won't regret it."

Isla sighed. He was like a dog with a bone. Or a bear with a whatever it preferred. "And a bear. A happy, smiley one. To make me a happy me."

"You'll always be you, a happy you when you're with me, I promise that. Whatever we do and however we do it. Will you give me a chance to show you?"

Isla didn't have to think twice. "Yes."

Am I out of my bloody mind? He could be anything. Worse than Julian or... Somehow, weirdly she knew he wasn't.

"Just like that?"

She grinned as once more the hot as hades bloke she'd first met stood in front of her. "Yes, with bells on?"

He laughed. "Yes, with bells on if you insist. I'd prefer you naked, but that can wait. Let's have fresh coffee, ring for a takeaway, and discuss how I'll turn your ankle into a work of art for a start. Okay?"

It sounded good to Isla. "Very. What sort of

takeaway?"

"You choose."

"Debby's Diner Dinner special. They'll need three hours, but it's worth it." Would he get the fact she was happy to spend all that time with him? She mentally crossed her fingers. This was all so un-Isla like, it would have—should have—been scary, but it wasn't. For the first time in ages she was happy and certain she was doing the correct thing.

He handed her his phone. "Would you mind? For whenever you prefer. Me? I'd say after we talk, I tell you and show you a bit about myself and if you're happy we make love, but that might be a wee bit late at night."

She let her breath out in a whoosh. He'd really said making love. Strange that it didn't seem too fast too forward or at all wrong.

"I'll say eight?" That gave them nine hours. Surely that would be enough?

Gaspar hunkered down in front of her, his impressive thighs straining the seams of his jeans. His eyes glowed, and once again she got a scent of wet animal.

"Aroused animal. All for you."

There she was getting those strange thoughts again.

"Not strange, pet. Just your mind beginning to open up and see what's going to be."

Shit, now her thoughts were coming in Gaspar's voice. "Er, Gaspar?"

"Yeah?"

"Oh, nothing. I'm wool gathering." How could she say nonchalantly, "Do you believe in shifters and stuff? Can you smell wet animal? Am I crazy?" She couldn't. Not without him calling for the men in the white coats.

"Hey, stop worrying." Gaspar moved her teeth from her lips and pressed a swift kiss to the bruised flesh. "You're not crazy, my pet. Just coming to terms with our future. Just like I did."

Okay now I am going screwy. I did not *say that out loud.*

"Are you a mind reader or something?" she demanded. Not that she believed in them either, but something was going on.

"Or something. You say you can smell wet animal?"

Isla nodded. "Yeah, not all the time but…"

"When I'm aroused," Gaspar said matter-of-factly. "Which is gonna be a lot more often now I'm around you."

That made no sense. "Yeah? Why?" Isla demanded. "Next you'll be telling me you're not really a human."

He nodded. "True. I'm a shifter."

Isla rolled her eyes. "Which of my mates put you up to this? The Isla reads all those books let's give her a taste of what she reads scenario eh? Early birthday present. So now what do I do? Tell you to show me? Ask if you're a wolf, a bear, or a squirrel."

He snorted. Then growled. He really did have the growl off pat.

Isla bit back her first frisson of fear. He sounded … pissed off. "Great growl," she said bravely and gritted her teeth and waited for him to respond.

His eyes glowed, and he opened his mouth to show fangs and … bloody hell. Impressive teeth.

"Oh yes," Gaspar said, his voice gravelly and guttural. "I excel at growling. And roaring, standing on two legs and giving my mate, my pet, my girl, all she desires. Which if my senses don't fail, is *us*. You and me.

My shifter self wants us to mate. Us to be a couple and us forever." He paused. "My human self wants that as well."

Fuck. Those words in his voice turned her to mush.

"After what, two hours or so?" Isla said in a swift, and unexpected, show of defiance again him. "Unlikely."

"Tut-tut, what was that I said about lying, my pet?"

Heat rushed into her cheeks. Was she going to get a punishment? Would he spank her? Would it be different from Julian's efforts? Did she want to find out, or was it time to say no thanks and goodbye?

"Gaspar, this is all happening too fast," Isla said in a shaky voice. "I've just met you. Yes, I'm attracted to you, but it's all too much too soon. Especially after." She waggled her leg so the horrible tattoo on her ankle showed. "After this. I'm scared. I'm not sure I dare open myself up again."

He hugged her tight, swung her up, and settled her on his lap. "How do you feel like this?"

Chapter Five

Gaspar held his breath as Isla wriggled over his rigid cock and almost made it break in two. Fuck, that was so erotic. So arousing and so bloody good. However, his dick now wanted to drill up her ass, and somehow, he didn't think she'd go for that right then.

One day he hoped but ... not yet.

"Like your cock is wanting in my ass," she said. "I don't do anal."

Bugger. Gaspar made a mental note to ask why and see if she'd change her mind at some point. In his mind, that slow, tight push into a hot as hades entrance, through tight muscles and then to sit deep and hard inside that secret place was one thing to be enjoyed above almost all else. The faith given to him not to hurt and the connection it gave was perfect. Even the thought of it made him ready to come.

Cool it. "Sorry about my dick. It's hot, hard, horny and eager to fuck with you. Okay, let me rephrase that. I'm hot, hard, horny and eager to make love with you. When you give me the go and not until. For now, though, horny cock withstanding, are you happy where you are?"

Isla nodded and wriggled again. "Ah that's better. Yep, I'm comfy."

Gaspar sure as hell wasn't. If his eyes weren't crossed they should be. "Okay," he said in a strangled voice. "Let's move on, to things we both need to know. First off. Do you trust me to sort your tattoo?" The sooner they got rid of the word Julian and changed it to something else the better. He had a few ideas on the bear and honeypot theme, but first he had to know, really know, she trusted him.

"Of course I do, I wouldn't be here else."

"Fair enough, then I'll draw up some ideas for you. Bear and honeypot, yes?"

Isla nodded.

"Second, are you prepared to try us for size?"

She sniggered. He laughed. "Yeah, that didn't quite come out the way it was supposed to. You know what I meant. We have a connection. One we both recognized instantly. One we'd be mad not to act on and see what it means."

"MacDonald and Campbell on the same side? The ancestors will turn in their graves."

He snorted. "There is that. Are you worried?'

"No, I don't see why I should. My Gran warned me when the right person came along there would be pitfalls and I'd need to keep an open mind. I'm not sure she meant the breaking of bread with the enemy so to speak, but hey ho."

He let out the breath he hadn't realized he was holding. Now for the next question. "This is a bit more tricky. What do you know and think of Doms and BDSM?"

Isla sighed. "That Julian wasn't one, that I didn't get what I should have. I was no sub to him, just someone to boss about without any thoughts for me and my wellbeing. Spanking fucking hurts, and is a major no go area, and scribing is another word for GBH."

Damn. Not as easy as he hoped. "Within a true Dom/sub relationship, it only hurts when it is mean to. Such as a punishment. For pleasure it hurts, it tingles, it morphs into something beautiful. And yes, I have been on the receiving end. I vowed never to do anything to my sub, I hadn't experienced myself. Anything," he stressed.

"Hmm," she said in a skeptical voice. "So you say. I'm not so sure."

Gaspar hugged her tight and stroked the side of her luscious breast. Her sharp intake of breath gave him hope. She wasn't unaffected, so maybe she'd be open to learning a little more? "I could show you, my pet. Show you what a really loving Dom/sub relationship is all about."

He hoped to hell his yearning didn't show in his voice. How Dom-like would that be? Uncertain and … fuck it, and human. "I hope I could," he added. "It's been a while. I swore I wouldn't let my Dom out to play until I knew it was with my mate. I've kept that vow."

Fuck and shit, why do I keep emphasizing the word "mate"? She'll ask why and then what? Bear comes out to play before time? That would put a right damper on everything. No human could be expected just to accept and understand. Fuck, even he had difficulty with the acceptance and understanding at times and he was born to it.

Isla stared at him. "You're holding something back," she said with more perception that he'd expected. "Open and honest at all times?"

He signed. "It sounds so far-fetched, you won't believe it."

"How do you know unless you tell me?"

She had a point.

"I am a shifter. Human into bear."

Isla blinked. "Oh, is that all? When you come or any time without warning?"

He guessed she didn't believe him then.

****

His eyes flashed, and by sheer force of will Isla didn't cringe or move away. After all who was she to say it could or couldn't happen? Whatever, she had no intention of asking him to prove it. That could come later. First, she wanted to get to know him in a more intimate, carnal way. Not only as a lover but also as a sub to his Dom.

So against her normal, clear-headed, think twice and then twice again before she made a decision, persona.

"Sir?" She slid to the floor and knelt in front of him, head bent. Her breathing sped up, and she did her best to calm herself.

Gaspar took her chin in his hands and encouraged her to look up at him. "Are you sure I'm your Sir, my pet?"

Isla nodded, no mean feat with her chin held fast. "Oh yes, Sir. Plea…please show me how pain is pleasure." She let out her breath in a whoosh. "I mean it, I want and need to know. Only from you."

The smile he gave her was all a woman could wish for. "Those words, from you, are heaven. Then follow me."

Gaspar took her hand and helped her to her feet. "We'll take it slow, my pet. Use the traffic light system. Red stop, yellow stop and let's talk, green all good and carry on. Yes?"

"Yes." Isla followed him into a small shadowy room, which held little more than a hard chair, a wide settee, and a three-legged table. "Cozy."

He laughed. "Not really but perfect for what we want. So, pet, are you ready to play?"

She grinned. "Oh yes, Sir." Ready was an understatement.

"Then, my pet, strip."

Isla blinked. He stood straight and stared at her. Testing her determination maybe? Was naked necessary? Maybe not, but if he wanted her like that, then naked she would be. Slowly, and with more provocation than she knew she had, she moved her buttons from their holes. A hiss of exhaled breath from Gaspar, the glitter in his eyes showed that he was aroused by her actions. Spurred on by that, she wriggled her butt and slipped her shirt off her shoulders to let it slide to the floor, then undid her bra and dropped it on top of the shirt.

"Fuck it, so fucking arousing and I'm as hard as a rock." Gaspar moved his hands to the snap of his jeans. "I need you, bare ass uppermost, across my lap, like now. Last one naked is a wuss."

Iona laughed and unzipped her skirt to kick it away as at the same time, Gaspar kicked his jeans off and pulled his t-shirt over his head. They shucked underwear together as if they were in synchronicity.

"Now, my pet." Gaspar sat on the hard chair and beckoned to her. "Color?"

"Green, Sir."

He let out a long whoosh of breath. "Thank goodness. Across my lap, please."

This was it. Isla counted to three. She could call red at any time. Carefully, and not without a lot of awkwardness, she bent down and wriggled until her clit rested across his thighs and her boobs hung pendulous and aching in the air.

"Like this, Sir?"

"Shit, Isla, pet, that is a sight to be revered and cherished," Gaspar said in a strangled voice. "All that would make it better is for those luscious globes of your ass to be red and show my handprint. Are you ready to see if I can take you to your special place? To show you how to fly. Ready to embrace the pain and let it flow into pleasure?"

"I am, Sir. Green and ready."

Brave words, and she wasn't so sure she meant them as the first, firm touch of his hand on her ass brought tears to her eyes. It did fucking hurt. The soft rub of his palm over the spot he'd spanked her helped a little, but... *sod it, I cannot cry red after one spank. I will not.*

"Okay?"

"Still green." Dammit, was she a wuss? Not anymore. "Really green," she added.

"Then count to five."

Smack.

"O...One."

Then that erotic stroke over her skin and... "Two ... three..." It didn't hurt, it stung. "Four ... five... *Oh*..."

"More, my pet?"

"Sir, oh please, yes, Sir."

He laughed softly. "Soon you'll fly, and I'll hold onto you, Keep you safe..."

Chapter Six

Watching his pet fly was the most cock-hardening, pre-cum inducing thing ever. Gaspar sat on the settee with his little subby curled up on his lap. He'd covered her with a blanket and made her sip some water and nibble some chocolate, before he'd cuddled her close and watched her as she murmured "nice … love…" and drifted off to sleep.

She might be all soft and comfortable. Gaspar certainly was not. His dick was still in fuck mode, his bear growling to get out, or at least mate and make her his, and every bloody nerve of his body screaming for release.

Comfortable—not. Content? Sort of. Determined to show her how they meshed? Definitely. Ready to take his time? Reluctantly. Gaspar rested his chin on the top of her head and wondered how the rest of the day would pan out.

However, there was one thing he knew and accepted. He'd wait as long as it took for them to be truly mated.

It wasn't that many minutes later before she stirred, blinked, and a slow smile spread over her face. "I didn't dream it, did I? You spanked me, I flew into sub space, and you held me until now?"

He nodded. "You were magnificent, my pet."

She giggled. "Good, but something is up."

"It is?" he asked, puzzled. "What?"

She slid off his lap and onto her knees and slowly, almost reverently touched the pre-cum slicked tip of his cock. "This is, Sir."

He laughed ruefully. "True, but it's not important. Your welfare is."

"Then, my Sir, my welfare will suffer if you don't let me do something about your state of … hardness."

Gaspar could hardly breathe. Did she mean… "What do you suggest?" he asked huskily.

Her expression was one hundred percent mischief. "May I show you, Sir?"

"Are you truly certain, pet? I don't want it to be senses overload or too much for you. We went deep, you're my perfect sub, and oh so receptive. I don't want to spoil it."

"Spoil it? Never." Isla said. "Sir, I know you may be wary of taking me when I'm probably still in sub mode, but I'm fine. I want to do this. *Can* I show you what I want?"

He nodded. "Be my guest." But he still looked worried. Isla was determined to show him what he meant to her. What they as a couple could be. It didn't matter she'd only known him a few hours; her body and mind accepted he was the one. And she allowed it seemed as if she'd known him for years.

"I'll say it once more, Sir. I'm green as grass sure. Or do I need to ask you what color you are?" she said with a smirk.

He laughed and tapped her smarting-in-a-most-delicious-way ass. "Green, you little subby Dom, you. Go on then, my pet. I'm all yours.'

Isla smiled and oh so slowly let her body slid down his, pleased they'd both undressed before her spanking. She gave up a prayer of thanks he'd suggested it.

"Then I suggest we start like this." She moved her finger, bent her head, and her mouth surrounded the head of his cock, just where her fingers had been.

****

Shit, fuck, and bugger. Gaspar saw stars, swore

his eyes crossed and his body went into spasms. Bloody, fucking amazing.

She glanced up at him, still with his cock held fast between her lips, and raised her eyebrows.

Gaspar nodded. He couldn't speak. Then he managed to croak, "Perfect."

She seemed to take that as an indication to go more and began to lave him. Her full lips firmed and softened in turn, and, impossible though it seemed, his dick became even harder. Fuck, he was about ready to come. But shit, he wanted to come in her, not her in him.

Gaspar tugged on her hair until she moved off him with a soft plop. Immediately he felt bereft, as if he'd lost something precious.

"I need to come in you, this first time," he said hoarsely. "Fuck you, fill you, and oh bollocks, no sodding condoms." He hit his forehead with his hand. How on earth could he have been so short-sighted?

Isla grinned. "Subby preparedness rule number one. In my skirt pocket. Hopefully not out of date." Gaspar swore he'd never moved so fast in his life. Within a minute he'd found it, used it, stretched Isla out on the sofa, and was poised to enter her.

"Fuck, love, I can't go slow, I'm almost breaking in two, ready to come and hell… bloody hell, are you sure?"

She'd taken hold of his cock, held him tight, lifted her hips and guided him inside her channel.

"Very sure. Now fuck me fast, my Sir. I need you."

That was one demand he had no problem with. Gaspar lunged deep into her cunt and began the ride of his life.

She matched him, push and squeeze until he knew he couldn't hold on any longer.

Isla screamed. "Now … argh. Yes, yes, argh…" Her voice trailed off as she sobbed. "Oh, oh, yes…"

"Yes," Gaspar roared the word, saw stars, and gave one last hard thrust and came. It was a wonder he didn't split the condom with the force of his ejaculation. "Mine. Mine…"

It was all he could manage.

Five minutes later, Gaspar did his best to get breath back into his lungs. He felt as if he'd run a marathon, backwards, with weights on his legs. Climbed the Matterhorn, danced the night away … or all of those together.

He felt fucking fan-tas-tic.

"W-wow," Isla wheezed as his softened cock slid out of her and he moved slowly backward to drop a kiss on her nose. "I'm wiped."

"My mate, you are magnificent."

"You were. That was…" Isla looked up at Gaspar. "Why are your eyes amber and glowing?"

"Ah. Hold on let me clean us up, we'll get dressed and I'll explain." Gaspar took hold of Isla's hand and walked into the tiny washroom and stiffened. *Hold on.*

Shit, we just did the beast with the two backs when anyone could have come in. Even though the room wasn't open to the shop he hadn't thought to lock the salon door.

"I bloody forgot to lock the door," he said gruffly. "Anyone could have come in. I'm not into exhibitionism."

"Nor me," Isla said cheerfully as she stood still to let him wash her where needed. "Just as well no one did then." She began to get dressed again. "I hate bras. We'll remember next time, eh?"

And that, he thought, was another reason to love

her. No recriminations, just a loving, "we'll remember next time".

"Leave it off, your bra."

Isla shook her head. "Not when I have to go outside. The girls are too big for that."

"The perfect handful." Gaspar tucked his t-shirt into his jeans. "Okay, coffee and confession time."

He led the way back into the other room.

"I'll never be able to look at this squishy sofa without going hot, cold, and all gooey."

He laughed. "Nor me, we might need to move it to our house when you come to me. You will one day, when you're ready?"

She smiled, and a gush of love filled her. "One day." She wasn't going to say soon, but she knew.

"Right then, you know when I asked you about shifters and if you believed in them?" Isla nodded.

"And I said I was one?"

"Yeah, so."

"Well." He didn't get any further. The shop door banged open, and two whirlwinds erupted into the room followed by a harassed looking woman who, Isla decided, had to be Gaspar's sister. The resemblance was obvious.

"My sister, Silvi," he said under his breath. "And my nephews."

The whirlwinds turned out to be identical boys of around ten years old. "Gaspar, you gonna shift and come play?"

"Not now, boys."

"Tommy, I told you." Silvi's voice was full of apology. "Never ask that in front of others."

"But, Mum, she's his mate, I can tell, so she must know. And anyway, Joey is, so why can't Gaspar?"

Isla looked from one twin to the other and gulped.

That child looked almightily like a bear cub … and hadn't Gaspar been inking bear cubs on that bloke's arm?

What if he was telling the truth? She'd made love with a bear? Fucked a bear?

Oh shoot.

No, not shoot… But what next?

"Joey, no."

The child turned and grinned. Tiny fangs, glowing eyes and claws. *Yeah claws.* The kid—cub?— stopped in his tracks and glowered. "But why not?"

"It's neither the time or the place," Gaspar said kindly, but firmly. "How often have you been told that? If you don't listen, learn and follow the rules there will be no shifting until you're of age. Get it?"

The half bear morphed back into a young boy, with tears in his eyes. "Sorry."

"Good. Remember to be and all will be well."

"I'm sorry, we only called in to invite you to dinner tomorrow," Silvi said.

Gaspar hugged her. "We'll be there, won't we, Isla?"

Did he sound worried. Isla made haste to reassure him.

"We will." She watched as the three trooped out. Gaspar followed, and she heard the snap of the shop door lock.

Isla swallowed and cleared her throat as Gaspar returned and stared at her, wariness uppermost in his expression. "Er, did I really see what I thought I saw? Is this for real, or am I dreaming? Pinch me."

He did, and she jumped. "Ow, that hurt."

"You asked," Gaspar pointed out.

"Yeah."

"So, can you explain that?"

He nodded. "I can, but will you believe me?"

"It depends. I kept hearing growls, and had no idea why."

He nodded. "Me, I dreamed of you. Heard you in my dreams and got hard and wanting." He cleared his throat. "Came in my dreams, but never ever saw your face. Then when you came into the shop I knew. It was you. My future."

"Aww." She looked at him, eyes wet. "That's so perfect. But why not my face?"

He shrugged. "Evidently it wasn't the time."

"Now it is."

Gaspar nodded.

"Thank goodness. I needed time to become me again. I'm so glad I did. You're everything I need and want, my Sir."

"I had no idea that the attraction would be so instant, so deep, so meaningful, or mutual."

She grinned. "Nor me. Boy, am I glad I saw your advert."

"You walked into the shop and wham. My bear told me. 'This is our mate. Our fulfilment'."

She grinned. "Even though I can't shift?"

He nodded. "Does that worry you? It doesn't me. You're mine. Our kids might be cubs or they might not. But they will be ours and loved. When you're ready I'm here for you, however you want. Mated, married, or living together. My wish is our wish."

"What more do we need?" Isla asked as she curled up next to him.

"Nothing. We've got all we will ever want need and desire. I love you.

"And I love you."

Inside Isla two little shapes stirred. Their parents might not know it yet, but they had them as well.

However they turned out, they knew they'd be

wanted and loved. Amazing what an unnoticed hole in a condom could do.

And they were.

The End

BARE ALLEY INK: VOLUME ONE

DEDICATION

To the RavDor Chicks. Thank you for all your help and support. You rock.
And to Paul, who is my rock.

BARE ALLEY INK: VOLUME ONE

THE GOOD BAD BOY

Bare Alley Ink, 2

Raven McAllan

Copyright © 2019

Chapter One

'Everyone loves a bad boy—don't they? Come and meet Chance…'

Gah, that was all I needed. Him twenty feet tall and his crotch at eye level. I glanced up at the poster and glared. Trust the local cinema to have his new blockbuster on soon after the premiere. That premiere was in four days' time and I intended to turn off every TV, radio, and app that might report it.

Bad in film, bad in life. That about summed it up. Dammit.

Noah Jackson's grinning face stared down at me, his baby blues taunting, teasing, and making me squirm. Not all bad, mind you, but not what I needed right now.

Liar, liar, pants on fire. Okay, then as I couldn't have him, for the last three years I'd had nobody, except Bill. Bill my bullet, that was.

Sadly, not Noah…

The open shirt, arrow of chest hair that enticed my eyes lower, the dark jeans unsnapped and...

Do not go there.

The poster was an advertisement for testosterone.

'Dark is the Heart *is Jackson at his best...*'

Sod it.

'*On at your local cinema soon...*'

Damn it.

Enough already, build a bridge get over it, move on, enough already.

He was in a past lifetime. As much as I wished he wasn't, he had to be for my sanity.

I shifted my glance from the poster to the street ahead. I was a clumsy sod and could trip over a matchstick with no trouble. Not a good thing in the main street, where no doubt I'd show my knickers to all and sundry. Which, as a local teacher, would so not be a good thing to do. No doubt half a dozen of my class would appear out of shop doorways with mobile phones in their sticky little mitts, snapping away and making my next term as embarrassing as hell. I shuddered at the thought.

Time to get my shopping and get the hell out of Dodge. I hated spending my days off shopping, anyway, especially the first day of the summer break, so this wasn't ever going to be my happiest of times, even without this latest crap.

Safety, in the form of a quick visit to the local deli for something tasty, and a good book called. Well away from the cinema, two-timing bastards, and stupid hot bod groupies who squealed like stuck pigs and made my life crappy.

Okay, a bit of an exaggeration, but blimey O'Reilly, as my mum would say, you'd exaggerate too if you'd been in my position.

Oh, I'm Summer, by the way. Hale, hearty, two

stones too heavy according to the doctor's scales, and fancy free. And, as I kept trying to persuade myself, well rid of Noah sex-on-legs Jackson.

Boy, how wrong could a woman be.

There I was lost in thoughts I didn't want, deciding on steak or salmon and sod it with chips, proper cholesterol-full chips, and I walked into a wall.

The wall swayed and swore and oh my, hands grabbed hold of my arms. Then hell's bells, I was lifted off my feet and held in the air, to one side of whoever it was. What was the world coming to? This was a main street in the city, only halfway through the afternoon, and no one but no one wondered what was going on. Well, no one except for me, and I had been too busy trying to regain my balance to wonder what on earth was going on.

I did my best to remember all those self-defense lessons someone had given me and kicked out as I went limp. Hallelujah, my foot connected with a shin. I heard a very pithy cuss word—*good*—and then I found myself touching the pavement again. Sadly still held fast, but it was better than getting motion sick. Mind you, if I had been sick, it might have been over the bugger who held on to me.

Time to scream? I opened my mouth and a big, luckily clean hand covered it. I bit. It did nothing to the bloke who held me. He just grunted. Sod and shit and fuck and bugger.

"Watch yersel, hen. Dinnae gie in th' way ae tha man."

"Why should she change the habits of a lifetime?"

Oh, shoot, I know that voice.

"Hello, Summer, my sunshine, how are you?" The deep, chocolate-smooth voice curled around my senses. "This saves us a journey."

Oh … bloody Nora.

Yeah, you guessed it. My nemesis was there in the flesh, not solely on a billboard. Okay, he had on those stupid shades and a baseball cap, which I always reckoned was a dead giveaway that someone was trying to go incognito, but it wasn't obvious who it was. Well, not to most people, I hoped.

"What do you want?" I said with a snap. After all, I was gradually being squashed and my 34DDs didn't like that. "Get the oaf to put me down before I shout GBH or something."

Noah Jackson, yeah, you guessed right, chuckled. "Put the lady down, Mac. I'll take over."

"Ah, ye sure, boss?"

Who the fuck was he?

"Yep, she's harmless. Aren't you, Summer?"

How I'd loved to have said no and thumped them both, but even in this not-so-big town in Scotland we were attracting a lot of attention, so I just nodded. "Yep."

Noah took my arm and sort of frog-marched me over to one of those stupid, mainly blacked-out windowed, top-of-the-range gas-guzzlers. "Get in."

I stopped dead and leaned on the side of the vehicle. "Pardon?"

He chuckled as the gorilla, sorry, bodyguard bloke, growled.

Growled, for fuck's sake. What, was he a bear?

"Summer, my love, before we attract any more attention, would you please get in? I really do need to talk to you."

I hadn't heard him sound so serious since … well, for ages. Even before everything went pear-shaped. I nodded and he held the door open for me to slide in and then followed me. The bodyguard slammed the door and got into the driver's seat. "Whaur tae?"

Noah glanced at me. I shrugged. "Home, I guess. You know the address." He gave it to—what was he called, Mac?—and settled back next to me.

"How are you?" Noah asked in his deep, gravelly, and bloody seductive voice. "You're looking good."

"Now, there's one thing I refuse to do," I said. "And that is talk to a pair of shades. Ditch the sunnies, and I might answer."

He laughed. "Forgot that, sorry."

Bless his little cottons, and I didn't say that about him often. He ditched the shades and those deep baby blues turned on me.

Sod it and be still my racing heart. The fucker still had me.

"So, my Summer sunshine, how are you?" he asked again. "I've missed you, and not just in bed." He sighed. "A certain part of my anatomy has forgotten how to grow and show, let alone what else it's supposed to be used for."

"Peeing," I said flatly. Did he really mean he'd been as celibate as I had? Seemed a bit implausible considering the circumstances, but I wouldn't challenge him, not now.

"Well, true, but nothing else. So, as I said before we got onto my urinary habits, how are you?"

Now how to answer that without sounding needy? "Fine," I said automatically. Well, I wasn't going to say, *I know what you mean about the bed bit and missing good sex and I've worn my bullet out now*, was I? It might be true, but oh, how it made me sound a loser. "You?"

He sighed. "Missing you."

"Yeah, right." Was it time to mention miss busy blonde costar who showed me the pictures? Maybe not. I sort of did the half smile if-you-say-so thing and he sighed again. He really had a good line in sighs.

"Oh, shut up," I said. "You weren't on the receiving end, I was." I thought about that statement. "You were on the direct receiving line, so to speak. It was your dick that was getting the action. I was just shown the photos." And even now the thought of those pics made me want to throw up.

"For God's sake, Summer, they were fucking doctored." He didn't sound angry, just defeated.

He'd said that at the time, but oh-so-insecure me didn't believe him. Now? Well, let's say three years older and wiser, and three years of dear Tawny Teesa's antics in every rag on the planet, I was prepared to be persuaded.

"So you said." Shit, what did I sound like? I was about to temper my reply when he got in first.

"Ah, what's the point? You'll never believe me. I have no bloody idea how to show you other than say so and expect you to accept my word. Just forget it." He sat back in his seat, folded his arms, and closed his eyes.

Oh, well done, Summer. I was actually disgusted with myself then. "I'm sorry, that didn't quite come out as I meant it."

He opened one eye. "No? Sounded as you meant it to me. Noah is a liar. End of." He shut his eye again.

As bad as sunglasses.

"For goodness sake, grow up and listen," I exploded. I mean, there I was about to grovel and do the benefit-of-doubt thing and he wasn't prepared to listen. A little voice in my head started to go on about, *well, why should he as I hadn't*, and I blocked it out. This was now, that had been then. "I'm trying to explain something to you. So if you want to hear it, open your eyes, sit up, and listen. If not, stop the bloody car and I'll get a taxi home."

He wriggled a bit, yawned in a way I had to bite my lip not to say something snarky, and sat up. "Okay, I'm all ears."

He might be all ears, but he still had his eyes shut. Ah, well, better than him staring and making me feel like an insect under a microscope. He was always bloody good at that as well, and I doubt he'd changed there.

Actually, I wondered how he'd changed at all.

"Summer," he prompted me. "Over to you."

"When we were together before," I said slowly, as I tried to say what I meant and get him to understand, "I wasn't exactly confident in, well, in what we had going for each other, and do *not* butt in, else."

He shut his mouth and inclined his head as he mimed a zip over his lips. That, of course, drew my attention to them and sod it, they twitched.

Chapter Two

"As I was saying, I couldn't believe someone like you even gave someone like me a second glance. I mean, you spent most of your time after filming miles away from me, which I know you couldn't help. I couldn't just up and leave uni to follow you around. So I went through agonies of worry as I saw all those photos of you with elegant, glamorous women in posh clubs, drinking champagne, and so on. There was I, a wee lassie from a wee village with no idea how to go on. I was out of my depth without a swim ring. Then there was your costar and her mates. Bitches all. Did you know I used to get special deliveries of copies of all the photos with you and her? Even the ones I would have seen in every paper? You were the flavor of the time and she was determined I was having nothing to do with you. Everywhere we went, she turned up. Innuendo in every gossip rag. And, of course, did you deny it? Did you hell. When I said it to you, you laughed it off. Just because you were filming together, you said."

Boy, was I on a roll. I knew once I started I wouldn't stop, but I hadn't realized just how much anger and yeah, sorrow, I still had inside me. "You screwed my mind good and proper and in the end, I just gave up. I said I couldn't cope any longer. I had my finals coming up, I was stressed to high heaven, and you just said it was part of life and to get over it."

He blinked. "Shit."

I nodded. "Oh, yeah, mega shit. Okay, I was years older than the rest of the students in my subject at uni, but in some ways, that put extra pressure on me. Doing a gap year or four across the globe might make you worldly wise, but it's not much help in a teaching degree. Well, except for the geography bit and most six-year-olds aren't that interested in the geography of New Zealand or Bali. It didn't help for the essay writing or the dissertation."

"Oh shit again. But you did well and got your job, though. Even if it was no thanks to me."

I shrugged. "I got the results the day you said I either got over my stupid jealousy or we were through. So we were through. I also got the pics of you and Tawny Teesa in bed. And you might say it was for a film, but oh boy, it looked remarkably like your bedroom to me."

"What?" He howled the word. "I never saw that."

"No? Ah, well, I did and I can tell you now it was the last straw. So I didn't come down, you got nominated for an Oscar, I got a job, and here we are." I glanced out the car window. "And here we are as well. Thanks for the lift."

For once, he looked a bit flustered. "Ah, can I come in, please?"

"Please? Blimey. Okay, enough of the sniping. I guess so." After all, hadn't I decided I was going to have an open mind? Well, sort of. "What about your goon … er driver?"

"Mac. He'll go to see his mum and stop there until I phone him."

I wasn't sure how I felt about that, but … new me. Sweetness and light until I found I needed otherwise. "Fair enough. Let's go in." Before the world and his wife—well, the farmer up the road, and the couple of blokes who lived half a mile away—wondered what the bloody blacked-out windowed car was all about.

****

"Why are you here Noah? Truthfully, no

bullshit."

We sat in the lounge and as ever, I realized just how big he was. Not fat but around six-four, a good foot taller than me, and in my tiny sitting room, he looked enormous. I did fear for my sofa before I remembered it was one that said all weights up to a combined fifty stones. That was at least twice the both of us. "I need straight-talking truth."

"Apart from needing a partner to my premiere? I've refused point blank to go with anyone but you. I went for a tattoo with Finn. Bare Alley Ink. Got a superb reputation."

I knew that. I'd been a few months ago and had the Chinese symbol for hope tattooed on my bum. Where it couldn't be seen, but I knew it was there. After all, we all need hope, eh? It seemed apt and well, I was too much of a wuss to go for anything else. How he'd coped with that great big one, I had no idea.

But I had other things to think about then.

"Finn? That reprobate?" Finn was his twin. "Shit, what did you get? Nekkid women dancing up your cocks?"

"Ha, ha, I'm not that brave to get anything in that region. He went for a bear up his side, and I went for a tiger. Look." He pulled off his shirt and turned his back to me. "Took several visits, which works well with me saying I was here with you."

Here? What the fuck? I went to answer and then stopped. My mouth went dry. It was a long while since I'd seen anything of him in the flesh, and oh God, my body responded like a bee to a flower or whatever the saying was. Let's say I went from cool, calm and sort of collected to hot and horny in three seconds flat. The sort of horny that made my nipples hurt and my thighs damp. Even my clit got into the act and began to throb. I hoped to hell none of my reactions showed. It was one thing to want to rip his clothes off and jump his bones, another for him to realize it. I swallowed and my bloody brain immediately remembered a different sort of swallow. Him. His cock and his cum.

Enough already. My cheeks were hot and I'd bet I had a sex rash spreading over me.

"Very nice," I said. *Oh, sheesh, can't I do better than that?* "It's amazing, but how the hell will you cover that up in a top-off film?"

"Clever people will do it for me. As it happens, I need a tat for the next one so it will be fine." He pulled the t-shirt on again, damn him. I had enjoyed the view. "Any coffee going?"

That was something about him that annoyed me. He could swap subjects as fast as, well, no idea what. I was going to say knickers but even I couldn't do that as fast as his trains of thoughts.

I pulled out the percolator. "Coffee coming up. I expect you want food as well?

"Well, now you mention it… What have you got?"

I tipped out my shopping bag. "You accosted me before I shopped so it's freezer food. Have a look."

He shook the bag and turned it upside down. "Empty."

"I told you. It's freezer rummage or a tin of beans."

"I'll rummage. Beans give me wind."

I knew that.

Noah opened my freezer door and began to move packages around. "Summer, what the hell is CCCWR42? Or, hold on, FPWP41?"

I sniggered. Well, I'd never expected anyone else to need to understand my labels. "Chili con carne with rice for two. Fish pie with prawns for one. There should be two of them. And if you find Paella shop-bought, I didn't make it. Nor oven chips or breaded fish."

Apart from veg, I reckoned that would be it. I'd not had time to stock up lately. Parents' evenings and end-of-term-itis had hit my class and every night all I wanted to do was have a glass of wine and sleep. Luckily, I'd eaten at school every day because there was no chance I would have cooked more than a cuppasoup and a cheese sarnie. "You choose." I bit back a yawn. "Sorry, I'm knackered. Today is the first day since whenever I felt I had nothing to do except nothing."

He nodded. I thought he'd get it. "I yearn for one of those days. I almost got one, except I'm here, I need you big time, and I'm not sure you'll play ball."

Now cat that I am, I liked that. "Maybe explain and I might?"

Noah muttered something that might have been okay and then came out of the freezer. "Do you have some meat and cheese?"

I thought about it. "Er. A bit of mild cheese might have mold on it, and a tin of corned beef?"

He winced. "Maybe not. Peppers? Mushrooms? Onions?"

"Well, duh."

"Then it's veggie pizza. With your stuff on it. Want me to do it?"

I'd had his doing it before. "No, ta, you pour the wine. White in the fridge, red in the pantry. You choose which."

We both had a glass of South African pinot noir. I added a bit of veg to the pizza and an hour later, we were, I hoped, both full.

"Have you thought any more about my needing you?" he asked.

Well, what a stupid question, I had hardly thought of anything else. "In what way and how?" I said in what was a cautious manner. I was still wary. "I'm not going tonsil to tonsil in public."

He almost spat his wine out. "Thank God. Summer, I need help. The film company is making noises about me not being in a stable relationship. They suggested the temper tantrum Tawny Teesa and I said no. I, ahem, also said my wife wouldn't like it."

Shit, fuck, and bugger.

Chapter Three

"How could you?" I was so taken aback to even think of something more forceful. "That's long gone."

"Not for me. We are still married and whatever you feel or say, I still love you. Always have, always will." His expression was unreadable. He'd always managed the inscrutable look well. "Sorry, but that's the way it is."

Sod him, he had the power to lift me up and sadly drop me down. "What did the powers that be say to that?"

"Where is she, why didn't we know, and what's her name? Amongst other things." He grinned and his eyes crinkled up. "I said, not here, no idea, and Mrs. Jackson. I thought one of them would have an apoplexy. Then I explained you had a career and we'd made the decision that it was fine for you to stay out of the limelight. That we met up without any fanfares and that was the way we like it. As I disappear to a cottage not far from here as often as I can, they couldn't dispute that."

I wondered if that was the Royal *we*. I guessed if he had to fudge the truth, that wasn't a bad effort, but I still had no intentions of being used as a prop. I might still fancy the pants off him, okay, no might, of course I did, but I wasn't going down the woman-when-I-get-five-minutes-to-spend-some-time-with route again. It was soul destroying.

"A cottage near here? And it's secret?" Shit, my voice had risen and I took a few hasty deep breaths. It was not the time for hysterics.

"Well, it's more of a barn on the edge of Simeon Cathcart's estate. You remember? I went to school with him and Heather, his wife. They know how to keep quiet."

No wonder I didn't know about it. Sim and Heather hadn't been backward at coming forward with their disapproval of what they called my lack of understanding. I had asked Heather how understanding she would have been if she was sent a photo of Sim in bed with a woman she knew wanted him, and I hadn't got much of an answer. She'd mumbled something about trust, but I could tell she wasn't as certain as she'd like to be.

Sim, on the other hand, was adamant I should accept what Noah said and if I didn't, he *was* going to take sides and it wouldn't be mine. And it wasn't. I hadn't spoken to him since Noah and I split. If I met them anywhere, Heather smiled and he blanked me.

"And of course I can always get Finn to run interference if need be," Noah went on, jolting me back to now and not then. "Sometimes it's handy having a double." He grinned. "Well, as long as no one clocks our tattoos."

That made sense. It was funny, though, how I'd never mistaken Finn for Noah. They might look the same, but to me, that was where any similarity ended. They were chalk and cheese. Finn was altogether too acerbic and temperamental for me to totally take to him. I supposed you could say we tolerated each other, no more.

Which had nothing to do with Noah and his request.

I was going to have to disappoint him. I daren't do it.

"Now you need someone to be what, arm candy? No can do. I'm not sweet enough." Not that it was the real reason, but it would do for now. I hoped he didn't question me too much. I wasn't an actor.

Noah laughed. "A nippy sweetie now, eh?" It was an expression we'd discovered both our mums used to describe someone who could give a sharp retort. I hadn't thought it applied to me. However, needs must and all that.

"You better believe it." I made the mistake of looking down. The bulge in his jeans seemed to be growing as I stared. I swear I salivated. Not a very sexy look. I probably looked more like I was constipated, but oh, shoot, how I loved to see that reaction from him. It sent me from cool, calm, and collected to hot and horny with damp thighs and those aching nipples in three seconds flat.

"Still do it to me, Summer. Can't help it. I want you and my cock isn't afraid to show it."

I might have guessed he would see where I was looking. "Well, it doesn't always get what it wants." I hoped to hell my baggy top hid my hard-as-nails nipples that I swear were boring a hole through the lace of my bra.

"I know that," he said in a rueful voice. "Oh, too well. But my need to be inside you, to hear those sexy and arousing little noises you make as you get excited, isn't what's important here. It's how you feel about me. Whether you'll help. And of course how much you'd like to metaphorically spit in Tawny's eye."

That got down to the crux of the matter. I would, of course. Who wouldn't? She'd made my life hell and it would be good to return the favor. But... And it was a very big *but*. At what expense to me? I knew only too well how Noah affected me and how easy it would be to get all-over affected again. And then what? It was bad enough when we split up last time. I didn't think I could cope with it all again.

"Summer, love? If it's too much to ask, just say so. I know I wasn't exactly supportive last time. I honestly didn't realize how bad it was until it was too late. And in the interests of honesty, I was so wrapped up in what I was told was a film that would make or break my career, it was all I focused on. I didn't realize what we had until I didn't have it." He swiveled to face me and took hold of my hands. "Can you ever forgive me? Honestly?" He swallowed deeply. "I'm not sure I can forgive myself." His grip tightened before he made a conscious effort to loosen it.

Oh blimey. That soft and sweet gesture was almost my undoing. "I don't know," I said. "I'd like to think I'm big enough to admit I could, could, mind you, have overreacted a bit, but she was so bloody convincing." *Plus, I'm a wuss.*

"And I wasn't supportive enough."

"That's about it."

I supposed it didn't really seem a lot to ask, but I hated being in the limelight. It was hard enough standing up in front of a class of twenty-odd six-year-olds, but at least I knew more about what we were discussing than they did. Well, most of the time. I'd admit I was a bit hazy about some of the up-to-date toys they talk about. I mean, I couldn't even keep my Tamagotchi alive, so what hope did I have with the latest Minecraft or whatever? Give me building bricks any time.

Which was me procrastinating again.

Think, woman. "What exactly would you want me to do?"

Noah pulled me into his arms, sat on the settee, and settled me on his lap. And that bulge, which now appeared to be trying to find a way through his jeans, my jeans, and any other clothing in the way. I wriggled, he groaned. It was such a sexy little groan I did it again, just to see what might happen next.

Noah held me still. "Stop it, love. I still need to be able to walk out of here with clean jeans. You carry on like that and there will be no chance."

Now contrary or what, I liked the sound of him being so turned on. Which wasn't fair, as I had no intention of doing anything about his hard-on. Or I hoped I wasn't. My willpower would crumble if he made a proper effort to seduce me. I knew that, and I hoped he didn't.

"Sorry." Half-true, anyway. "You were going to tell me what you needed me to do."

"Come to the premiere with me. Be seen around with me every so often. Be my wife, be known as my wife. Show we're deeply in love, have never split up, and laugh if anyone tries to say Bloody Tawny Teesa—which is as stupid a name as she is—were ever an item. If she tries to fling, I say that metaphorically, those photos at you, yawn and say, thank goodness photoshop has moved on since those amateur days, and generally be amused at her antics. In public, anyway. In private, we can make voodoo dolls and throw darts at her face on a dartboard or whatever turns us on." He did a very over-the-top leer. "Especially the last bit."

"In your dreams." And mine as well, but that was privileged information and not for sharing.

"Oh yes. Every night, love. So?"

"Do you honestly think we could carry it off?"

Chapter Four

"Why not?"

"I'm no actor," I said for the umpteenth time.

"Why act?" he said.

He seemed genuinely surprised at my question. Well, he wasn't looking at it from where I was.

"I'm not all horrible, am I?" he asked. "I don't smell, I clean my teeth regularly, and I am nice to animals and old people. I love you, even if you don't believe it. I like you as well. It won't be all on show, I promise. Just the premiere and a few other bits and bobs."

It was the bits and bobs I worried about. Oh, the premiere would be scary enough, but at least I could watch the film and no doubt grit my teeth when he made love to bloody Tawny. Even if it was as he reiterated, all make-believe.

"What are they then? The bits and bobs?"

"Go to Cheltenham for the Gold Cup, maybe Formula One. A few things like that where we can be on show without having to put on too much of a show."

"Wimbledon, England-Scotland rugby?" I asked hopefully. I'd guessed I might as well add a few things I'd like to do.

"Your wish, my love, if at all possible, will be my command."

I had to bite my lip not to say *hot as hades sex here and now*. I'd become more and more aroused by the minute. Luckily, not enough to ditch all common sense.

"When would we need to start?" I said, resigned to the fact that common sense or not, I was going to help him as best I can.

"We've started."

"Eh?" I asked, a bit startled by that comment. "How?"

"By going to the pub for a pint. Come on. Let's live dangerously."

That was coming out as a couple with a vengeance. "Out of character, maybe?"

"We can say we're celebrating the fact I've finished my film and we both have a few weeks off."

I had six, as it was the first week of the school holidays. Which made me think of something. "You said Cheltenham? That's next year."

"So is the rugby," Noah pointed out. He hugged me. "Let's play it all by ear."

****

Which was how an hour later, hand in hand, we'd sauntered along the lane toward the Champion public house. My local which, to be honest, I only went into on occasion. Like end-of-term nights out with a couple of my co-workers and when there was a village do on I felt I ought to support. Even our school, pupil numbers seventy-three, give or take five, depending whether the Mackie family were living here or Tenerife, held fundraisers in the back room. I'd never mentioned who my husband was, just called him Joe—his middle name—and said he worked away a lot. Noah wasn't the only one to have lied over the years. Whenever I didn't get out a lot, I said we'd been having quality time together. People generally thought it was ever so romantic that we didn't want to share our time together with other people. If a few people wondered if it was a mythical husband, no one chose to say so in my hearing.

If nothing else, this would get the gossips going. I wasn't sure I liked that thought, but as my mum would say, build a bridge and get over it.

"God, I'm scared." I blurted it out as we crossed the bridge over the river and headed for the pub a few yards away. Why it was called the Champion and not the river was lost in the annals of time. Something to do with a horse and a mountain guide. *I think.* No one seemed to know the whole story.

"What on earth have you to be scared about?" Noah sounded genuinely perplexed. "It's just a pint or a glass or two of wine."

"Little you know about it. It's open to all who I am, and with you. Get ready for gushing. Oh, and the *what the fuck does he see in* her?"

"What crap." He sounded genuinely astonished. "I'll sort anyone who dares say anything in my hearing."

It was outwith his hearing I was worried about, but I didn't think I'd say that. Life was about to become interesting.

We passed the local shop.

"Do we need anything?" Noah asked. "Wine, cheese, chocolate?"

"Probably all three," I said. "Plus a bucket of courage." I was due to do my monthly trip to the big supermarket in town that week. Today's visit had been a quick nip in and out on the local bus. My use-it-or-lose-it trip that we were all urged to do. Actually, I enjoyed the bus ride as much as I disliked the supermarket, which I put off as often as possible. "The cupboards are about bare."

"Let's go into the shop then." He held my arm in a fierce grip. "They do the first three, I'll give you the last."

"I don't know I…"

He clucked. The bugger did flappy arms and made chicken noises.

I punched his stomach and burst into laughter.

Noah took advantage and propelled me into the shop. Imaginatively called The Village Shop.

"So, love, what do we need?" He put his arm around my shoulder and kissed the top of my head.

Argh, the sickly smile and loving grin made me bite back a snigger. Talk about over-the-top.

"Wine, cheese, and chocolate," I said as I suppressed the urge to make sicky noises or stick my tongue out. "Chenin, Edam, and dark."

He turned to old Mrs. Black. Shop owner and the number-one gossip of the village, and probably not that old. It was just what she was called to differentiate her from the other two Mrs. Blacks in the village. Her job was perfectly suited to her purpose in life. To find out as much as she could about as many people as possible. "As my wife said."

To say her eyes nearly fell out was an understatement. "Oh my goodness you ... you're," she squeaked and patted her hair. I had no idea people did that in real life. I thought it was a romance book thing. You know, they see a hot bod and pat their hair and lick their lips. Thank goodness she didn't do the latter. I really would be making sicky noises then.

"Summer's husband," Noah said. "Call me Joe." He winked. "I let close friends call me that."

Mrs. Black stammered, took his hand, and shook it so much I thought he'd have a bruise.

"Oh my, oh yes, well, yes indeed. Let me..." She swallowed. "Let me go and get your shopping. What is it?"

"Wine, cheese, and chocolate," I said again. I thought it was about time I reminded her I was there. "But we can get it ourselves."

She looked at me as if I was an alien who had sneaked into the shop unseen. Well, I supposed in her eyes, I was unseen. Just as well I found it amusing. It could be, as I knew from the past, very demoralizing to be invisible.

"Oh, Mrs. er, Jackson … I er…"

I took pity on her. "Summer will do."

"Summer, oh such pretty name, and you want, yes, well … I'll get what you need."

She stopped talking and went to the cheese cabinet. Anyone would think she'd never seen me before. I'd lived and worked in the village for almost three years. Mind you, in all that time, she'd never offered to help me get my shopping, or as far as I knew, anyone else. It was usually a case of walking the two tiny aisles and getting it yourself.

She put the largest piece of Edam I'd seen stocked there on the counter and looked at Noah. "I'm no wine connoisseur, Mr. er Joe… You choose."

Noah gave his professional smile and Mrs. Black almost fell into a puddle of drool at his feet. "I'll let Summer choose it," he said. "She knows what we both like."

I also knew we had a choice between two, neither brilliant but both quaffable. I picked up the one I preferred, which weirdly was the cheaper. I was sure it was underpriced because I'd checked it on my wine app, but there was no way I was telling Mrs. B that.

Noah glanced at it, and then me. I did a tiny nod, and he nodded back. "Great, hon. Right, so just chocolate and we're good to go."

"Oh yes, my… er, this one?" Mrs. Black put down the bar I usually bought and beamed. "Are you sure that's the lot?"

Noah looked at me. "We good?"

"Yep, that's it."

"Then this, and a shopping bag please."

I stood back and waited for Noah to pay, Mrs. Black to simper, and me to manage not to giggle. I could see Mrs. B was trying her best not to ask Noah if he was any relation to Noah Jackson, and I wondered if she'd manage it. If she did, I bet I'd get the third degree next time I went in.

By the time we got outside, I was wondering just what I'd let myself in for. I mean, hot to trot was an understatement. I couldn't be near him and not be affected—damn it to hell. One of his unconsciously smoldering looks and I was toast. If he touched me behind my ear or nibbled the lobe I was a goner. My mind went into overdrive as I remembered just how, and where, and how often we'd made love. And believe me, it was making love, not just sex. I knew the difference.

Now, I thought he did as well. Because if he didn't, there was no hope for us. I was *not* going to settle for second best. I deserved more, and okay, so did Noah.

The expression *pants on fire* wasn't far wrong. To want for a better expression, if he played his cards right—or even wrong—one of those looks and I'd be ready, willing, and able. Or his on a plate.

Mrs. B seemed to feel the same.

If it was like that with Mrs. B, God help us in the pub, or even worse, in the big wide world. No wonder he'd spent a lot of time on Sim's estate and introduced himself to Mrs. B as Joe. His Noah persona would be known soon enough if he insisted on me accompanying him to what I called posh frock dos.

"Nice lady," he said amiably. "Very attentive."

"Well, duh. She'll give me the third, fourth and fifth degree next time I go in."

"Ah well, such is life." Noah swung the carrier around in a circle. "I could say welcome to my world again, but I don't want to put you off before we get started. Seriously, though, Summer, I do appreciate all this. It won't be all bad, honestly. Once the first throes of nosiness are over, interest will die down."

"If you say so." I wasn't convinced, but I wasn't going to go back on my word. Apart from anything else, I wanted to see his film and I might as well do that from a comfy seat. The fact I'd have to watch a larger-than-life Noah making love to bloody Tawny, I intended to forget about. I could always try to remember my new timetable for the next school year, or recite the two-times table, and do the cloudy-eye-keep-them-open-but-not-look stuff.

"What are you thinking?"

Chapter Five

We'd reached the pub garden and were heading for the door. "Eh?" How the hell does he always ask that at the right time? Do I have one of those bubbles coming out of my head with the words *I am thinking* in it?

"You, you're worrying I can tell." Noah stopped walking. "What about?"

Should I tell him? I took a deep breath. Why not? "Watching you and Tawny on the big screen."

He roared with laughter, to the extent tears were at the corner of his eyes.

"You *what*? Oh, hon, apart from acting, I ate garlic so she didn't overstep the mark."

I rocked on my heels. The visions that conjured up. "You what? Tawny the vampire?"

"It wouldn't surprise me. Then if I thought she was taking liberties, I breathed heavily all over her. Plus, I grew my fingernails. They got dug into her a few times before she got the message. Actually, I did her a favor because she winced and hissed once or twice and it looked like she was in the throes of ecstasy. The director was very impressed."

It was my turn to roar with laughter. "Oh, I love it." And I'd remember it when I needed to. "When is this premiere, by the way, and why are you looking shifty?'

He coughed. "Moi?"

"Yes, you. Come on, Noah, truth time. Today is Monday, and the poster in town says the film is on here from Friday. So?"

"Thursday."

"Thursday?" The screech I gave made even me wince. Three pigeons flew up and away in a hurry, and Lager, the pub's tortoiseshell cat, which had been heading in our direction, turned tail and headed back the way he came. "Shit, Noah, and between now and then, I need to get a dress, get defuzzed, have hair, nails, and God knows whatever else done. Give me a break."

"I did. I almost left it until Wednesday and kidnapped you."

Just as well he hadn't, I'd have killed him.

"Never fear, though, all is sorted. If you're agreeable," he added hastily. "I've got it all in hand."

That was what I was worried about.

"Sorted as in how?" I asked once we'd picked up our drinks and decided to sit in the garden. It was sunny and breezy, but by unspoken agreement, we'd decided to go outside where we could talk and not be under a microscope, so to speak. I'd forgotten all these sorts of things. Guess for a while I'd have to remember them.

"Sheesh, I thought it was going to be twenty questions in there," he said as he rested his chin in his palm and spoke softly without moving his lips much.

That was something I hated. "Is this cloak-and-dagger talk behind your hand really necessary?" I asked, doing the same thing, damn it.

He leaned forward so our noses were almost touching. "Dunno, but I bet you a quid someone in there knows it's me and either has their phone cameras on us or is gonna come out and ask. After all, they know you all as Mrs. Jackson, don't they?"

Fuck and bugger, I hadn't thought of that. "Point taken." I gave in to impulse and made sure our noses rubbed together. Noah stuck his tongue out and touched my lips. My nose twitched. Before, that would have led to lots of interesting things that would get us arrested if we'd attempted them in the pub garden. "Do we drink up and go, or suck it up and see?"

Noah glanced over my head. "Looks like it's the

second. Incoming couple at three o'clock. Follow my lead. I bet my hut on the estate is sounding ever more appealing, eh?"

He had a point.

I watched as he straightened, held on to the hand I didn't have curled around my wine glass. That was so no one could see it shake. Confrontations or meetings like this made me feel sick.

Noah began to speak. "So, of course we can decide about the paint color later," he said with an almost imperceptible wink. "I still like the gray, but your eye is much better than mine. We'll check the charts, eh?"

"Yes, why not, there's no hurry," I said and wondered what else to add. "Better to wait and be certain."

"Er, Mr. Jackson?" Two twenty-somethings stood at the table. One was the mum of one of the girls in my class, the other I didn't know. Pam, the mum, and I went to the same ballet class for adults.

Noah leaned back and glanced up at the newcomers. "Yes?" he said politely. "Can I help you?"

"Hello, Pam," I said to the mum of Diane. "All ready for the holidays?"

She looked at me as if she'd never seen me before. "Oh, Summer. I didn't see you there, sorry."

"Story of my life when we're together," I said in an amused—at least I hoped it sounded amused—voice. "I'm used to it."

She reddened. What a cat I was, and I *liked* Pam. Ah, well, I'd explain when I got the chance. "Anyway," I added. "You wanted to ask my husband something?"

"He really is your husband?" the other woman said in a disbelieving voice.

"I really am," Noah said. "Thankfully. So Pam and?"

"Eloise, and Mr. Jackson, I'm so glad to meet you," Eloise gushed and sat down next to him. Noah moved away slightly and his lips twitched.

"Thank you, nice to meet you both as well."

Gah, I hated gushers. No not the sex gush. Though for ages, I didn't believe in that and now I do. No, I wasn't going into any more detail. Use your imagination.

"I've seen your films and I wanted to say that you…"

"Ellie," Pam snapped. "At least have the decency to ask if you can sit down and if Mr. Jackson is who you think he is and if he and his wife mind having their valuable time together interrupted." She turned to me and mouthed, *She is a PITA*. "I know Summer says they have little enough time together as it is."

I snorted and changed it into a cough as Eloise's eyes widened so far, I thought her false eyelashes might fall off. "You mean you knew?" she said to Pam. "And never told me, your sister? You bitch."

"Takes one to know one," Pam said. "And let's face it, Ellie, you couldn't keep a secret if your life depended on it. If Summer and her husband don't want their relationship broadcast to all and sundry, I'll do my best to help them."

"Thank you, Pam," Noah and I said together as Ellie scowled.

"Welcome, Joe."

He, bless him, took his cue. "It's like you say, how often do we get a chance to wander out like this? We're making the most of it." He waved his pint in the air. "And we better drink up or dinner will be ruined." He drained the rest of his beer at a pace a Guinness Book of Records holder would be proud of. "I'm cooking, so I need time to burn stuff. Ready, hon?"

I'd been sipping my wine all through the exchange so I had no need to gulp much down. I swallowed the last drop and stood up as well.

Eloise looked at Noah. "Joe? She called you Joe."

Noah nodded. "My friends do."

"Oh." I could see she wasn't sure whether to ask anything else.

"Come on, Ellie, we were only supposed to be here for half an hour. The men will be going mental with all the kids and no beer." Pam waved her carrier. "That was our mission and for Ellie to have a crafty fag. See you at ballet on Thursday?" she asked as they began to walk in one direction and us in the other. "Last one before the summer break."

Noah looked at me and I know he was giving me the option to answer why I wouldn't be there.

I took a deep breath. "Actually, no, not this week. It's the premiere of *Dark is the Heart*."

Chapter Six

I could hear Eloise moaning as they walked away, and Pam saying something about, "Why should I tell you? Grow up." I could have kissed her. I must remember to give her a proper explanation when I could.

"Blimey, what a..." I hesitated. "Over-forceful woman."

"Yeah, so you really are coming? To the premiere?"

"I really am," I said. "As long as I get everything done. I refuse to go continental with hairy armpits or an upper lip moustache."

Noah almost dropped the shopping bag. "The pictures that conjures up. Well, I've got two options for you. Mac can take us to London tomorrow and we do everything there, or we sneak into Glasgow, if need be. Meanwhile, I have an option on two dresses for you from Leisha the new English designer who's taking the fashion world by storm, and they can be couriered up to your house or mine on Sim's estate. Likewise, Heather says she's happy to do whatever you want her to. Don't forget she qualified in everything you'll need except the makeup and nails, and you'd be better getting that done down south anyway."

"Up here and Heather," I said immediately. "As long as Simeon won't mind." And I thought there would be no need to go into Glasgow either. I'd gotten my holdy-in knickers nicely worn in and no way was I buying new ones that might give me the right shape but not let me breathe or drink fizz.

"Sim is an idiot and I've told him so many times," Noah said robustly. "Ignore him. I do."

That sounded good to me. "Then your house? Because once the jungle telegraph has got hold of the fact Joe is Noah, I bet I'll have an awful lot of people passing by." I'd got visions of everyone from Mag the postwoman to Tam the coalman knocking on the door for some trumped-up reason or another. "Like soon."

I had a thought. "Do you have two bedrooms?" There was no way I was jumping into bed with him. Well, no, let's be honest. I wanted him to think that and persuade me otherwise.

"Yes, Miss Suspicious, I do." We walked briskly home. Once there, Noah wandered into the kitchen and opened the fridge door. "Shall we take the perishable stuff?"

"Might as well." I headed for the stairs and my bedroom. How long would I need to pack for? What the hell was in the wash? "Do you have a washing machine?"

"All mod cons. Grab what you need and I'll ring Mac to pick us up. How long do you need?"

Forever. "Give me half an hour."

He laughed. "I'll say three quarters."

Cheeky sod.

"I bet you, half an hour." I grabbed my suitcase and began to fling stuff in it. I could nip back if I forgot anything—or buy new. I was nothing if not innovative.

I dashed into the bathroom, saw my pills, and shoved them into my sponge bag. They were something I couldn't manage without. Not that I was sure we might get down and jiggy, Noah might not want to, but better to be safe than sorry.

I dashed down the stairs somewhat out of breath with three minutes to spare.

Noah appeared from the kitchen like a jack in the box. "Well, my sweetie, go you. I am impressed."

"Shades of a teacher's life," I said. "Timetables, always timetables. So, what now?"

"Mac will be outside in a couple of minutes. I told him the back lane. Less chance of being waylaid."

Sometimes my husband was so sharp he'd cut himself.

"Clever."

As we left by the back door, I heard the front doorbell. "Is that saved by the bell?" I asked as Noah opened the back gate with the code I gave him, locked it behind us, and a long dark-windowed car glided up. I'd never realized how useful this admittedly rough but handy lane was. About two hundred yards further on, it went into a farmyard used by the Forestry Commission, and nowhere else. But for us today, as a blessed shortcut that bypassed the village, it was perfect. I guessed it took a long way round to where I thought Noah's house—*barn? shack?*—was, but if it meant we got away without anyone knowing, it was all fine by me.

Mac turned around and grinned as we got in. "Runnni' awaw?"

"You better believe it," I said. "I need time to get into role."

Mac guffawed. I'd forgotten that people ever made that particular noise, and oh now it took me back. "Lassie, you'll be fine. Won't she, Joe?"

So Mac called Noah Joe as well. Interesting.

Noah nodded. "In every way possible. But for now, let's get home, and we can sort out more details."

I approved of that. I was a quivering mass of insecurities, so any help would be welcome. "Lots more details."

Mac laughed again. "Mrs. Summer, just go with the flow."

That would help if I knew what the flow was.

Noah grimaced. "I've thrown her in at the deep end. I think I need to offer a viable plan of happy action."

He could say that again. I nodded. "Yep, you better believe it."

Mac grunted. "Ahm just the driver."

Noah laughed. "Get away, man. But okay, I'll do the plot, and you better be able to carry it out."

Mac muttered and turned down the sort of track guaranteed to give you nausea. This area was covered with them, but I mostly walked or cycled on them and missed the worst of the ruts. A car was hard pressed to do that. I swallowed several times and counted to ten. There was a reason for this route, so I had to suck it up. Luckily, before I gave in and threw up, we stopped.

"Welcome to my humble abode," Noah said.

I stared out the car window. Humble, my arse. It might be a barn, but it was twice the size of my cottage and I bet ten times as opulent. "Your idea of humble and mine are a bit different," I said as I got out of the car. "Like by a hundred percent." Even so, I was looking forward to seeing inside.

"Well, it was a wreck the first time I saw it. Still had animal crap, and I mean that literally, all over it," Noah said. "It took me three weeks of hard labor, all by myself, to clean it. Then I worked out what I wanted." He cleared his throat. "What I thought we would want. I lived in hope you'd come here one day and like it as much as I do."

Aww. Now how to reply?

"Well, I think it is gorgeous from the outside and I can't wait to see inside," I said. "But don't blame me for anything."

"I won't. Shall we have a cuppa? Before we go see Heather and find out what's what?"

I nodded. Anything to delay Simeon's

disapproval.

As ever, Noah seemed to understand my thought progress. "He's loyal, Summer. Don't judge him, he saw the state I was in. Heather saw further and tried to say so were you. But to him, you didn't even try to see my side of it, even though I told him the circumstance. Hell, I would have been like you, but to Sim, it was a no-go, and in the end, Heather and I agreed not to say anything to him. He has high blood pressure."

Shit, that was all I needed.

"Well, don't make it higher cos of me."

"No fear. I think he gets it now. If he doesn't, Heather might shoot him."

How to install confidence in twenty seconds—not.

"I think I need that cuppa." Wine might be better but I reckoned I better keep a clear head.

Noah opened the front door of his barn and stood back to let me go in.

Gobsmacked was an understatement, believe me. The hall was wide and airy and went from the ground up to the roof, which was a long way. The staircase wound around one side and I could see a long landing with doors off it. I itched to go and be nosy. In front of us, three doors were ajar.

"Kitchen, lounge, dining room," Noah said as he propelled me into the kitchen. Behind us, I heard Mac grunt, and presumably drop my case, before he shouted, "Ahm off," and a door closed with a *thunk*.

Just us then. Shit. All of a sudden, I was uncertain again. It was all well and good having deluded myself that I was over Noah, that I could cope with being around him and not want to jump his bones when we *weren't* together. Not so easy when we were. Every nerve end was on high alert—if that was possible.

Noah switched the kettle on.

"Time for a guided tour while we wait for it to boil?"

Chapter Seven

"Why not?" After all, I was itching to see upstairs. What red-blooded woman wouldn't? There was something so arousing about the way a man decorated his own personal space. Plus, if he'd hoped I would come here one day, would it be all masculine or would there be something softer that would appeal to me?

Noah took hold of my hand. Was I being fanciful and imagining he stroked it with his thumb as we left the kitchen and peered into the lounge and dining room and cloakroom? Well, if I was, it was a bloody rousing imagining. Talk about tingles and shivers up and down my spine. Rock-hard nipples again, and yeah, something that sounded so bloody ridiculous I hardly dare say it. What Heather once described as a quivering clit. We'd both gone into fits of giggles when she said that. I mean, talk about flowery, purple prose. However, now I honestly knew what she meant even if I thought it could be described differently. I wasn't sure how, exactly, because let's face it, damp knicker-making doesn't conjure up a pretty picture, does it? But I reckon you'd get the gist.

By the time we got to the top of the stairs, I could swear my heart was racing, my knees knocking, and my mind buzzing.

Noah pushed open the first door. "Guest room and en suite." It was pretty but nothing to write home about.

"Very nice."

He laughed. "Bland and safe. Just like spare room two." He indicated the next door.

It was true, and the only difference was one had

blue accessories and one lemon.

"I hope this is a bit different." Had his voice deepened, or was I hoping? My pulse jumped as Noah pushed open the next door and stood to one side.

"Decorated with us in mind."

I took a deep breath and walked the few steps so I was inside. Looked around and burst into tears.

"Summer? Love?" Noah was after me in a second. "What's wrong? Shit, I thought you'd like it." He hugged me and well, I had to hug him back.

"I love it," I wailed. "It's everything I want with you."

I felt him stiffen and then sigh deeply. "With me?"

I sniffed. No more hesitating. "If you want me?" I rested my cheek on his chest. I was home.

Noah stretched his arm out and grabbed a tissue from a box on the most gorgeous antique chest of drawers I had ever seen. "Blow," he said. "Then say that again please."

I blew and looked around for a bin. Noah took my snotty tissue from me and dropped it in the bin I'd missed seeing. Now that had to mean something, right? I mean, someone else's snotty tissue wasn't a nice thing to hold even for a second.

"I want you if you want me," I said. "Utterly and truly."

"Really? Just like that? No strings or explanations?"

"Really," I confirmed. "Just like this." I gathered up all my courage and kissed him. Proper, lip-locking, tongue-meshing kissing. It was far too long since I'd done that.

Wow. Just definitely nipple-tingling, clit-quivering wow.

Noah groaned, I moaned. He moved one hand to my breast, I moved one hand to the zipper of his jeans.

Then it was a mad fumble and scramble to see who could get who naked first. I had no idea who did, but within seconds, we were both in our birthday suits. Noah flung the duvet back with one hand then picked me up and dropped me in the middle of the mattress.

It made me giggle as I bounced and he scrambled to flop down beside me.

"Oh God, Summer, I've dreamed of this."

I didn't get a chance to answer. I was too busy trying not to come as he kissed and then sucked my nipples, and saints above, began to play with my clit. Oh Lordy, so bloody good. I think I moaned, but to be honest, I was drowning in the sensation so I had no idea.

Somehow, I managed to find his cock and stroke it. It was Noah's turn to moan now.

"Fuck it, I want to be in you. Need to be in you, and I've no bloody condoms." He moved away a bit and I took advantage of the fact to get onto my knees, take his cock into my mouth, and lave it.

Not a boy scout then.

"On the pill," I mumbled around a mouthful of hot, hard, but soft as silk, male flesh. "Clean, and fuck it, fill me." I took one long hard pull on his dick and let go with a plop. Better than an ice lolly any day.

Noah didn't hesitate, thank goodness, and had me on my back and his cock poised at the entrance to my channel faster than I could say *climax*.

"Got to be now, love."

Just as well.

He pushed. I clenched my inner muscles—thank goodness for Kegel exercises—and held him tight. Noah swore and laughed. I grinned and we set up that age-old motion of in, out, tighten, release until I felt him swell even more inside me.

My nipples hurt in the best possible way.

"Sheesh, now got to be, oh Lord, help please…" I was almost incoherent, sobbing, throbbing, and any other *ing* you could mention. It was pleasure, it was pain, it was…

"Now!" Noah roared, and his hot, sticky release filled me.

"*Yes.*" I let myself fly and saw stars as my climax hit me with all the subtlety of a baseball hit by a champion.

Yeah, I was a screamer. Did I care? Not one bit. I moaned, groaned, and wriggled as well. Loved it all.

Loved Noah.

Bloody hell, I hoped I didn't say that out loud. Not yet, anyway.

He beat me to it.

"Love you, Summer. Always have. Missed you, so, so much." His voice was slurred.

Had he fallen asleep? I squirmed around a bit so I wasn't totally squashed and squinted up at him. For someone who sounded half-cut or totally sated, he appeared reasonably bright and alert.

"I mean it." He raised himself on his elbows and as his cock slipped out of me, he rolled over and took me with him.

"Never let it be said that I, as a gentleman, let you, my lady, be on the wet bit."

Actually, it wasn't wet, just a wee bit damp, but hey, I wasn't complaining. Noah tucked me tight next to him and I put my arm over his middle with a happy sigh. This was how it should be and sod anyone who tried to make it different. Then my mad would come out with a vengeance and then heaven help them. No more a doormat, no more a scaredy cat, now a tigress.

I hoped.

"I love you as well." I guessed I sort of mumbled it into his armpit—weird, yes, I know, but my face wasn't that far away from it—because he tugged on my hair.

"Say what?"

I couldn't really say *you heard*, because I didn't know if he did. Anyway, a declaration of love should be heard, shouldn't it?

"Noah Joseph Jackson, I love you. I trust you and fuck anyone who tries to come between us."

He grinned. "The only fucking either of will do is with each other."

I spluttered. Trust him. "Well, yeah. You and me."

"'Til baby makes three?"

He stroked my cheek. I melted all over again.

"One day." I wanted time for just the two of us first. "But not yet."

As he always had, Noah understood what I was saying. "Sounds good. Think of all the fun we can have practicing." He moved so his hardening cock rubbed my belly.

I pushed myself up to kiss his nipple. "Maybe we ought to start now?"

Epilogue

We went to the premiere. He got a standing ovation. I got a series of scowls from Tawny Teesa, whose name Noah told me was really Freda Smith. She did her best to get Noah's attention and failed miserably.

I watched the sex scenes without a blink and had to hold my laughter back when Noah whispered in my ear, "See? That's the garlic," and a bit later on, "Nails used there."

We had a laugh about how we'd had our tattoos done at the same place and talked about maybe us each getting the same one in the future.

We met up with Simeon and Heather, and although Sim was a bit stiff with me at first, over the weeks and months, we'd got back onto our old footing. Finn was his usual self, but hey, I could, and did ignore him.

As for a family? Let's say I'm waddling well, and the way whatever it is kicks, he or she could be the next Scotland—or I suppose, England or Ireland star. Of course, I say Rugby. Heather is all for a cricketer and the men say football.

But to be honest, be it a boy or a girl, we just wanted a healthy, happy baby who does whatever he or she wants to do.

As for Noah and I?

Happy was an understatement. Mind you, when he was filming sex scenes, I still checked he'd had a stash of garlic and long nails.

The End

DEDICATION

To the Chicks,

Without you this story wouldn't have been written.

Many thanks :-)

BARE ALLEY INK: VOLUME ONE

THE PUKES' CHRISTMAS ABDUCTIONS

Doris O'Connor and Raven McAllan

Copyright © 2015

Chapter One

Haversham House, Christmas Ball, December, current time

"Good lord, I need a minute. How anyone could breathe with these freaking stays on, I have no idea."

Clara gasped for breath, and rolled her eyes at Vicky's smirk. Her new-found friend looked as fresh as a daisy, *dammit,* whereas Clara was sure she was going to pass out soon, if she didn't get these torture objects off of her.

"Wuss. I told you, many ladies in that era didn't bother with stays but you insisted." Vicky rolled her eyes. "Your fault. Me? I had more sense. Hence I didn't wear any under my costume."

Clara grimaced anew and looked pointedly from her heaving cleavage to Vicky's nice tidy handful.

"You get away with that. Without scaffolding of some sort I'd be wobbling all over the place even more than I am now. My boobs are too damn big."

"Rubbish, and the girls are perfect for a Regency dress. Let's face it, my 34 As are blink-and-you'll-miss-them nonentities. Why do you think I have a supply of chicken fillets and tissues all over the place? A becomes C. You know full well most women would kill for your cleavage. As for stays … overrated. Hell, Clo, I didn't even put a chemise underneath ... you know," she added at Clara's blank look, "a sort of petticoat under a petticoat. That coal sack you're wearing, and complaining it chafes your pussy. At least in Regency times they weren't rough and coarse if you were aristocracy, but still, I guess in this day and age you have to get what the costumier thinks is authentic. But hey it's no wonder you're overheating in that get up. Bet you still got your knickers on too, right?" Her impossible friend, who was enjoying herself far too much at her expense, giggled. "I haven't. What's the point in daring to go bare, if you cover it all up? We need to get you out of those awful things you call knickers. In the meantime…"

She paused to snare two flutes of champagne off a passing footman, and pressed one into Clara's hand.

"Bottoms up. You'll feel better once you've had another drink." Vicky winked at her, and grimacing Clara downed the lot in one go. She wasn't a huge fan of the bubbly stuff, but it did lubricate her throat, and left a nice buzz behind. Well, either that, or the lack of oxygen to her lungs was making her this fuzzy headed.

"Are my ladies quite all right?"

James, Haversham's resident butler, swooped in with his usual majestic grace. It always left Clara feeling somewhat inferior, which was ridiculous. She was curator of this great house, after all. Yet next to the whitehaired, impeccably mannered James, whose family had been butlers in this house since the beginning of time—if he was to be believed—she always felt like an imposter. He certainly never looked at her with the great respect he bestowed Vicky from the minute she'd arrived.

"Lady Victoria Hopewell, my pleasure to welcome you to Haversham House." The voice wasn't actually unctuous but not far off. Luckily her friend had held in the giggle Clara was certain she wanted to give and apart from the twinkle in her eyes, showed no surprise at the greeting. Instead she got into the spirit of things, bowed her head, and murmured her acquiescence. Only, once he was out of earshot, she'd dissolved into fits of giggles.

"Goodness, he does take this whole Regency authenticity to the extreme, doesn't he? No one ever called me Lady Victoria before, or if they have it was so long ago I don't remember."

"Yes, well, that's James. He's just one of the oddities that surround this house. No wonder their previous curator left. The poor man probably gave himself an ulcer working around the impossible demands placed in the will of the last Duke of Hockwell."

Vicky nudged her in the ribs and gesticulated. "Shh, he's waiting for us now."

Clara watched wide-eyed and full of envy as her friend drew herself up to her full height of around five feet seven. She even looked like a member of the aristocracy who would have graced this elegant house two hundred years ago.

"I say, James, would you be so kind as to show us to the withdrawing rooms for the ladies?" Vicky's stilted accent shook Clara out of her musings about the state of Haversham House, and focused her attention back on her friend.

James's lined face broke into a wide smile, and he bowed again.

"Certainly, my lady. If you follow me to the gallery, you will find private rooms off there."

Vicky grinned and grasping Clara by the elbow, hissed in her ear.

"Gallery, eh? That's pictures and portraits of the family. Does that mean he's taking us to the private wing?" Clara had to smile at the excitement in her friend's voice.

"That means chamber pots and stuff, or is there a loo there?"

"There's a loo." Clara smiled at the look of disappointment that spread over Vicky's face. "You don't really want to pee in one of those gravy boat things you showed me, do you? Isn't that taking authenticity a bit far?"

"I guess but..." Vicky punched Clara on the arm as Clara howled with laughter. The noise echoed around the gallery and Vicky shh-ed her. "Stop it," Vicky hissed. "You'll get us black balled. No don't." Clara sniggered and snorted until tears ran down her cheeks. Vicky tried to be stern and didn't make it. "Oh Clo, shut up or you'll start me off."

"B ... black ... balled. I thought lack of sex was blue-balled and okay, I've zipped it. Just look around and remember stuff."

This would be excellent research for Vicky's next historical romance, after all, and had been the main reason why Clara had ensured Vicky had received one of the coveted invitations to the Christmas ball. They were usually reserved for the cream of society. With a glance back at the crowded ballroom, Clara allowed herself to be led away, satisfied that the evening went as planned, even if the supposed heir hadn't turned up.

In truth, she was quite curious to see the private wing too. James and his wife, the resident cook and housekeeper, kept the keys for this wing. Clara was due to catalogue all the items in that part of the great house soon. She hadn't managed to do so yet, her attention taken up with the parts of Haversham House open to the public, and thus paying her wages. Which, should the estate not sort out this missing heir to the dukedom issue, wouldn't happen for much longer.

James stopped outside the imposing oak paneled door, and unlocked it with great flourish. A strike of lightning lit up the dark interior before the lights came on, and Clara jumped.

"It seems the predicted storm is approaching faster than anticipated. If my ladies will excuse me, I'd better make sure our guests are taken care of."

James inclined his head, and before Clara could get over her astonishment at the fact that James was leaving them on their own in this sacred part of the house, Vicky had pushed through the door.

With an impending sense of doom, and accompanied by a loud clap of thunder, Clara followed into the dimly lit long hallway. The heavy door clicked shut behind her. Goosebumps broke out on her skin as the temperature instantly dropped, and she rubbed her hands up and down her exposed forearms.

Vicky, who by all accounts ought to be shivering in her barely there outfit, jumped up and down in excitement.

"Wow, look at all these old paintings. These must be their ancestors, and I have to say these two don't half look yummy. Cousins it says. I think they've got the same great grandfather. So there's a bit of a gap, you know second cousins once removed or something,"

Vicky said as she peered at the metal tags on the frames. "But, boy, you can tell they weren't born on the wrong side of the blanket. Come here, have a look."

Vicky waved her on, and with a sigh of foreboding Clara stepped forward. The entire hallway lit up in a blinding flash as she did so, and the most enormous rumble of thunder deafened her. Vicky screamed and darkness descended.

Someone or something brushed up against Clara's back, and she barely suppressed a shriek. She hated the dark with a vengeance, at the best of times. Through the driving rain lashing against the windows now, she heard the sound of a match being struck.

"Deuce, Kit, where the devil are you?"

Spinning round to the sound of that deep masculine rumble, Clara lost her footing as the rug on the floor gave way. A strong masculine arm snaked around her waist, and hoisted her up, against a broad, warm chest. Scents of horse, tobacco, and some woodsy cologne teased her nostrils, as the unknown invader lifted up the lone candle, placed in an old fashioned candle holder, seemingly to study her.

"What have we here? I'm not sure what game my cousin is playing, but I think I shall keep this bounty."

The man, who looked as though he'd stepped straight out of one of those paintings smirked, and raised one perfectly shaped blond eyebrow at her. A flash of lightning made the diamond in his cravat sparkle, and the ring with what looked like a crest on his pinkie shine brightly in the dim candlelight. He bowed from the waist and took her limp hand in his, to kiss it suavely.

"Daniel Danvers, Duke of Hockwell at your service, Miss...?"

Pressed against him as she was, Clara couldn't breathe, couldn't think, and for the first time in her twenty five years swooned like a good old Regency heroine.

****

"Tarnation, Dan what the hell are you playing at?" Christian—known to all except his mother as Kit—Capel, the Duke of Aulban, swore as he turned from another candle he'd managed to light, to see his cousin holding a swooning woman in his arms. "Who is she?"

Daniel shook his head. "In truth, I have no idea but she's a pretty handful. The storm blew out the candle and, well…" He shrugged and shifted his grip on the swooning woman to lift her into his arms. "I got one lit and here she is."

Kit shook his head. "Just like that? So which debutante is she? I must admit this is a new way to ensnare a duke. Wait for a storm, blow out the candles and sneak into the private wing. Thence to be compromised. Welcome to the world of the leg-shackled man."

Daniel glowered. "I've no idea who she is but it matters not. It won't rub, no leg shackling will occur. I'll deny it all. After all I was with you all evening."

Kit grinned. "Of course. As I was with you. Just in case Marianna Allencroft claims otherwise."

Daniel paused on his way toward the door, which led to his rooms. "Fair Marianna?" He whistled. "You lucky dog. How was it?"

Kit considered. "It would have been bland. I scratched the itch once before, but that was it. She of course was more than satisfied, but I had no intention of returning for another course. Once over egged dish was enough." He shuddered. "She wears so much attar of roses I was almost the one to swoon the time I did partake."

"Poor man." Daniel's voice was mocking, and Kit

snorted.

"I assure you 'tis true. She got to taste my pudding and I declined to sup her nectar."

Daniel kicked open the door. "Only taste, not enclose?"

"I decided enough was enough. The woman ate me like she was starved." He paused. "Although if the gossip mongers are to be believed, Alllencroft isn't, shall we say, able to perform. Too many dubious encounters in Portugal."

"Poor sot. I suppose I could say poor Mariana but … I can't say I've ever warmed to her." Daniel walked through the open door. "Now this handful could be something different."

Kit stared at the unconscious woman in his cousin's arms. Much too voluptuous for his liking, but definitely to his cousin's taste. "I wish you joy."

"I wish me cunt."

****

Vicky listened with growing anger as the two impeccably dressed men talked so callously about women. Okay they might have found the perfect costumes but did they really have to make their performance quite so authentic? Men—well some men—had moved on surely?

The door banged behind her friend and the first guy and she jumped as she realized she was stuck in the semi dark with an unknown man. One who hadn't clocked her yet, but it was surely only a matter of time before he discovered he wasn't alone? Vicky groped over the shelf of the mantelpiece she'd found in her fumble along the wall once they'd been plunged into darkness. Clara had been several yards ahead of her, and in the eye line of the two men. Luckily, Vicky thought, as she was behind them, her presence hadn't been noted.

Where had they appeared from? She could have sworn she and Clara had been the only two in the room when the lights went out.

Wherever it was now she not only had to contend with a storm, and boy she hated storms and always had, but also a drop dead gorgeous, play your cards right and you can have me guy in front of her, and her friend god knew where with this guy's almost double.

It was enough to make even the hardest woman swoon, and whatever others might think—and her last boyfriend insisted he knew—Vicky was no ball buster. Oh she was an outspoken, in your face feminist, and had long thought women got a raw deal at times, but she also knew given the right man she'd roll over and purr. Unfortunately Maurice—hedge fund analyst and all out asshole—Endon hadn't been that one.

The guy in front of her lifted the candle he held high in the air and turned in her direction. Vicky bit her lip, slid her hand a few inches further and to her utmost relief touched something cold and hard. She almost groaned her relief out loud. Thank god for small mercies. It might only be another candlestick but it was empty, heavy, and available. As a cosh it would work as long as she had the element of surprise. If it bent and wrapped itself around the bloke's head it didn't matter as long as it gave her time to find Clara and they both got away unscathed. Vicky decided she could bet her new iPad mini these two weren't the sort to kiss a hand and say good bye.

More like kiss somewhere else and demand more.

The man in front of her turned and stared straight at her. His blond hair glittered gold in the candlelight and his blue eyes matched the color of his impeccable evening jacket that sculpted his body. He flexed his long fingers, which gripped the candlestick. Vicky's mouth went dry. That small gesture made her think of how they would grip her. How he would grip her.

She swallowed as an unholy grin spread over his face and the corners of his eyes crinkled up.

Well," he drawled. "It seems it was indeed a lucky day I told Lady Allencroft enough was enough, and I preferred to partake of supper elsewhere." He walked purposefully toward her. "And lo and behold my supper is waiting. Neat and perfect for me." He stared meaningfully at her breasts.

To her chagrin Vicky felt her nipples tighten to the point of pain … or nipple clamps in place. Then her sex-hazed mind cleared, she processed his sentence and her blood boiled. How dare he suggest she was on the menu? She gripped her unlit candlestick harder and waved it in the air. "You come near me, mate, and I'll knock your brains out. And as most men's brains are in their gonads be prepared to sing soprano from now on in."

He blinked but didn't miss a step.

"I don't sing. Not for anything including my supper," he said as he reached for her.

Vicky moved sideways and lifted the candlestick above her, ready to strike.

A flash of lightning was followed almost immediately by a clap of thunder

Vicky screamed and threw the candlestick in the air. Something—someone—grabbed her, and then the candlestick swung around in lazy circles high above her.

Almost in slow motion both she and her assailant watched it fall toward them.

Her last thought was it would hit her not him, and try as she might she couldn't move.

I hate storms.

Chapter Two

Daniel whistled to himself, as he shouldered open the door to his rooms. This fragrant bundle of curves in his arms would prove a fine distraction away from the tediousness that was the annual estate Yule Ball. The servants enjoyed the one night they could join in the festivities, though it made for dashed uncomfortable lodgings for him.

Jenkins, his valet, was no doubt romancing Bella, the kitchen maid he was sweet on, having been given the evening off, but you'd have thought they'd have made sure to light the fires in his rooms.

In the flash of another lightning bolt that lit up his sitting room he could see his breath curl in front of his face, and the lady's lips were turning blue.

Cursing under his breath, he abandoned his plan to do the gentlemanly thing and put her down on the overlarge and overstuffed armchair in front of the fire. If he had to light his own blasted fire, he would do so in the comfort of his bedchamber. Just as he feared the hearth in this chamber was stone cold also, but the room was marginally warmer, no doubt due to the long, south-facing windows, now covered with deep maroon velvet.

His captive moaned in his arms. It wasn't a happy sound, but a distressed, strangled sigh which made him deposit the dark haired siren in the middle of his four poster bed. With one strike of the tinderbox, he lit the oil lamp, adjusted the wick, better to see, and pulled in a sharp breath. Her hairpins had come out and the mass of her dark locks framed a face he was certain he had never seen before. The freckles dotted across her nose, testament to a life spent not shading herself from the sun, as any lady would, and that, as well as the inferior silk used in her dress confirmed his suspicion. This was no debutante, or widow of the ton.

Most likely this minx was one of the newer servants he hadn't come across yet. Perhaps a lady's maid, who had liberated one of her mistress's cast-offs to enable her to attend this ball. It would also explain why she seemed unable to breathe. The gown had clearly been designed for someone less voluptuous than his find, and in an effort to fit into it, the silly chit had laced herself too tight.

Only one thing for it, put his skills to good use and liberate the *lady*. With practiced moves Daniel turned her on her side, undid the tiny buttons down the back of the dress, slipped it off her shoulders, and then slid the material down her body. His cock stirred at the sight of her curves held in by the corset. The ribbons of her rough cotton chemise were caught in the ties of her stays, so he simply ripped the fabric, and sliced through the ties with the hunting knife he'd found next to the oil lamp.

It was a curious place to leave it, and Daniel couldn't recall having done so, but it certainly came in handy now. His intended sport for the night pulled in a shuddering breath when he yanked the stays off, and the now tattered chemise followed suit. Daniel grinned as her luscious breasts fell free. Delightfully large and heavy, the globes sported wide areolae and big nipples which stiffened under his gaze. Sadly not due to his presence, but the cold in the room, and Daniel swore again and shrugged out of his dinner coat to cover the girl up until he could get the fire started. Half in, half out of his tight fitting jacket, which was a devil of a job to get off without Jenkins, he paused and gaped.

What on earth was she wearing on her cunt?

Some contraption with images of what looked like a dressed up bathing sponge with a face. Whatever it was, it was an abomination to his eyes, and far more importantly spoiled his view of what he would find between her legs.

Adjusting his prick with a rueful grin at that organ's single minded intent—it had been way too long since he last indulged—he placed his coat over the seemingly still unconscious lady. Something like a gasp escaped her lips when he did so, and Daniel frowned down on her. Her eyelashes fluttered against her cheeks, and moving her arms out above her head the girl stretched like a cat waking up from sleep. She blew out a breath. It ruffled Daniel's hair and brought with it the scent of warm, fragrant woman, a hint of whatever she used to wash her dark locks, and the fruity flavour of whatever punch they gave to the servants.

"Vicky, 's zat you?"

The sleepy words came out slurred, and Daniel shook his head. Halfway to being foxed, no doubt, which would go some way to explaining why she had been wandering around the private wing. No servant would set out to snare a duke, after all, but a servant girl, overwhelmed by the ball, the drink, and perhaps urged on by a sweetheart or a friend … yes, she could well have lost her way. Fortunate for him.

With one last searching look at sleeping beauty on his bed, Daniel turned to light the fire. At least it had been well prepared and all he had to do was strike the tinderbox. Once he got a good blaze going, he turned to find his prey awake. Eyes wide, his evening coat clutched to cover her nakedness in a white knuckled grip that would have Jenkins curse at the creases on the morrow, she appeared to vacillate between looking him up and down, flinching at the flashes of thunder and lightning, and looking for an escape. Her teeth sank into her lush bottom lip, and she looked ready to bolt, when he approached.

"Wh-who are you?"

****

The man slowly walking in her direction frowned at her and Clara wanted the ground to swallow her up. This could not be happening to her. Clara Ellington did not wake up in a strange man's bed. A man whose astonishing blue eyes lit up with definite male appreciation as he let his gaze slowly run over her body.

When he bowed and grinned, that smile lit up his rough features, revealing laughter lines around his eyes. Her traitorous hormones sighed in bliss at the way the roaring fire lit up his silhouette through the fine linen of his dress shirt and accentuated the muscled body underneath. Lean hips, powerful thighs, and polished knee high tasseled boots she was sure she could see herself in if she bent down—this stranger was the very image of Regency aristocracy, which must mean she had either lost her mind … or she was ... *dreaming*.

Clara blew out a breath of relief. Yes, that had to be it. It had been one hectic week after all, getting everything ready for the ball. She got all hot and bothered, she remembered that, and Vicky had taken her…

"Where's Vicky?" she asked.

The stranger crossed his arms over his chest, cocked an eyebrow, and shrugged his shoulders.

"My dear chit, I do not know of any Vicky. What sort of a name is that anyhow?"

Clara bit the inside of her mouth to stop herself from rolling her eyes. Dream or not, this fellow didn't look as though he would appreciate such a gesture. Instead, she sat up a bit straighter. Her scant cover slipped and she realized with a start that she was naked, apart from her favorite boy pants underwear. Guess that explained why she could breathe again.

"Vicky, my friend. She was right there with me in the gallery, when...."

His amused laugh stopped her.

"The wine you indulged in addled your brains, girl. There was no one there but you, me, and Aulban."

"Who the hell is Aulban?" she asked, and swallowed nervously when his amusement fled as quickly as it had appeared. *Should that be who or what? Have I put my foot in it?*

"Look, girl, as appealing as you are, this subterfuge stops now. You know fine well who Kit—Aulban—is. What I want to know is who you are, and what the deuce you're doing in my house."

Clara's head started to hurt again. Had he said his house? With a sudden clarity of vision she recalled the events leading up to her losing consciousness, and her heart beat faster.

"Your house? Hardly. I'm the curator, and I should be asking you what you're doing..." The words dried in her mouth when this far too handsome stranger took the diamond pin out of his intricately tied neck cloth and started to unravel the material from around his neck.

"What are you...?"

"It's getting nice and warm in here now, girl, and as I will clearly be working up a sweat, trying to get the truth out of you, I'm going to make myself comfortable." His smile was sin itself when he reached behind him and pulled his shirt over and off his head in one fluent move. Before she even had a chance to appreciate the display of fine male muscle in front of her, the bed dipped, and the world tilted. Robbed of the cover of his coat, she found herself dumped over his knee, arms and legs flailing, before the first swat to her ass made her screech.

"Scream all you want, girl, but no one will hear you. The truth now."

Another much harder swat to her ass took her breath away for a second, and she tried to push herself off his lap. His arm across her shoulders stopped her, however.

"I can do this all night, girl. Tell me the truth. Curator indeed. This is Haverham House, not a museum."

Clara shook her head in a vain attempt to clear away the lingering moth balls. Not helped one bit by the infuriating man now stroking the tender skin on her behind. That felt way too … *nice. Oh, god, if he keeps that up, he'll soon discover how wet that is making me.*

Even in her thoughts that seemed wrong. Clara might enjoy her naughty stories, the naughtier the better, but things like this did not happen in real life. Which left only one logical conclusion. She *was* dreaming, because the only other alternative was that she was losing her mind. Just to test the theory, she screamed.

"I'm not lying. I'm ouch. Vicky. *Vicky*, where the hell are you?"

****

"Clo…Clara… What…." Vicky felt herself ruthlessly shaken as her friend's scream echoed through her brain. God almighty her head hurt and her mouth was as dry as a desert. What the hell had happened?

"My heart, wake up, come back to me." Someone patted her cheek none too gently and she tried to swat the hand away. Her head hurt enough without a sore cheek added.

Her hand wouldn't move. She tugged but whatever held it, held it fast.

"Victoria." The voice was enough to make her

pussy tingle, her muscles tighten, and her nerves quiver. "Stop that at once."

What the fuck? Vicky opened her eyes slowly and squinted at the dark, saturnine, shadow in front of her, silhouetted by the light of a seven-armed candelabra. Nothing stood out except two grey eyes with golden glints that danced in the candlelight and beckoned to her. Deep, dangerous, hot as hell... *Hell?*

She tried to scream, she really did, but her vocal cords seemed to have frozen, and nothing emerged except a tiny croak. Not the thing to stop Satan in his tracks.

She bucked her ass in the air. As she'd wondered, only her ass moved. Her legs were held as tightly as her arms.

"What the fuck?" That came out okay. Vicky shook her head and blinked. The shadow moved again and got closer. She wished she could shrink into herself or at least hide under the covers. "Don't you come any nearer, buster. You've got a helluvalot to answer for. Get talking fast. What the hell am I doing trussed up like a BDSM offering?" She glared as best she could with a brass band playing inside her skull. She might like a bit of consensual pain when she was in the right frame of mind, but this wasn't consensual and she sure wasn't in the proper mindset. She wasn't even sure what set her mind was playing at.

"Silly woman, what are you talking about? BD whatever? I have no idea what you mean. Stop struggling or you'll hurt yourself." His voice was as smooth as liquid chocolate, as dark as the night, and as enticing as anything she'd ever heard. Her pussy juices began to make their presence known to her.

God, stop right there. I am not gonna gush in front of a devil—or Mr. A. N. Other dressed up as one. If only she could clench her thighs together, but of course spread eagled as she was there was no chance. Vicky bit her lip in an effort to control her body. She wasn't sure she managed.

"Please, who are you?" Hell, now she was begging. She might sub as the mood took her but meek and begging didn't come into her remit. Ever.

He moved the candelabra to one side and the light shone fully on his face. It was enough to set her pussy throbbing like a damn pile driver. He was everything she ever wanted in a man. Tall, with short blond hair, dark eyelashes and eyebrows and grey eyes that shone and sparkled like the sea on a sunny winter's day. Her libido jumped to attention, and the throbbing in her head decided to give it a break and become more of a hint of a headache than a full on pain. He smiled.

"Victoria, enough is enough."

Victoria? No one called her that if they valued their body the way it was. It might be a family name but Vicky hated it. Ever since the school bully had teased her with 'Victor-eah, has gonnor-eah, don't go nee-ah.' He didn't carry on with his death wish words after she'd kneed him in the balls and added, 'Bobby Mollock's got no bollocks'.

"Victoria?" The man's voice hardened. "Look at me and answer me. What's all this nonsense?"

She recognized him. Sort of.

"You're the guy in the portrait I was looking at when…" She faltered, swallowed and cleared her throat. Things began to fall into place. Horrible, scary, that what the fuck is going on place.

"God I hate storms. Where's Clo? And who was that guy who abducted her?" Her words tumbled out in a rush. "Why have you tied me up, what's going on and Aghhhhhhhh." A flash of lightning and a loud clap of thunder made her freeze and to her utmost shame and horror she began to sob.

Shit I hate me like this, but godalmighty I think it's inevitable. Not in a scene in a scene. *At a sodding fancy dress ball in a bloody storm and no duvet to hide under or cat to cuddle. I hate storms.*

" I hate storms."

He moved swiftly. "Oh my heart I know you do. If you promise not to thrash around anymore I'll unfasten you. I was so scared you'd hurt yourself."

He, dammit she needed to know his name, she couldn't call him *him* all the time, moved to her side. "Yes?"

"What? Oh right." She remembered his statement. "No thrashing, though I might hide under the duvet and shake. I..."

"Hate storms." He bent to the ties at her feet and unfastened them with a speed any Dom in the club she visited would envy. "So you say every time. Before you grab Corso—the kitten," he added evidently in response to her blank look of query—"and head for the silverware cupboard and usurp the butler." He repeated his actions on her wrists and lifted her into his arms. "This time you have me. We'll shut the curtains and cuddle."

Vicky decided she liked the sound of that except for a few important points she'd just discovered.

"I'm naked."

"I like you naked," he said, unconcerned as her voice rose to ear splitting screech-level once more.

God knew she'd probably have lost her voice before long if she didn't calm down.

"You might, but I don't go naked with someone I don't know." There, that sounded reasonable, didn't it?

"You don't go naked with anyone except me or I'll tan your sweet arse until it's the color of those curtains over there." He pointed to the long, deep red curtains that dressed the floor to ceiling windows, which showed the rain lashing on their panes and every so often allowed the room to brighten up with lightning, and dim the glow of the candles. "You're mine, *ma petite*. Only mine. And with me, only me, you are naked."

"Hmm. So you say. Then if I'm yours, who am I and who the hell are you?" She glared at him, and waited to hear what he would say. Something else niggled at the corner of her mind. "Why did you call me that?"

He raised one sculpted eyebrow in a most imperious manner. Something that she rather thought would normally reduce her to acquiescence.

Normally? What on earth is normal? "Why did you call me ma petite?"

Chapter Three

Kit bit back the oath he wanted to utter and counted to ten. Why on earth was his usually biddable, well biddable as long as it was within the dynamic they had agreed on, or in the sphere of their everyday life, wife acting like a spoiled young deb? She knew fine well what his uttering of *ma petite* meant.

Didn't she? Her strange behavior worried him, and that query worried him most of all.

When he'd met his Victoria and told her of his likes and needs she'd listened wide eyed and thought for several minutes. Then she'd tilted her head to one side and smiled. "A *dynamique*? Something we wish to have and adhere to?"

He grinned and tapped her backside none too gently. "Exactly. So we have a dynamic of our own for us and us alone, and a life on show to others. But if I say to you *ma petite,* you know it is our special time. Yes?" She'd nodded.

Now he wondered if she really had suffered a stronger injury than he originally thought.

"Victoria I'm beginning to fret more than a little." He settled her deep into his lap so his cock was squashed between her arse cheeks. "Why are you denying all we have? All we are?"

She gave him the sort of look guaranteed to shrivel bollocks. All of a sudden he was glad his were hidden under her body and his evening breeches.

"Maybe you could get it into your pea brain that I haven't a scooby what you're on about?" she suggested.

Kit understood sarcasm when it was delivered in that tone of voice. It was a pity he had no idea what she said. "It's now established that a brain isn't the size of a pea." Well he was sure he'd read that somewhere.

"In a male, considerably smaller?" Victoria suggested sweetly. "And in a man's case located in his gonads?"

His lips twitched involuntarily. "Gonads?"

"Bollocks."

"Ah. Well let me just say some of your phraseology is incomprehensible to me."

"Eh? Oh good grief. Let's converse in words of two syllables eh?" She shivered. "And pretty please with sprinkles on, can I have a robe or something? Why don't you have the heating on?"

He gestured to the fire. "It's as good a blaze as ever."

"No, the…"

He watched as she looked slowly around the room.

"Is the electric off cos of the storm? Clara said it does happen sometime. But I thought you'd have lamps and things, not just candles."

He latched on to the one sentence he understood. "We decided only to use candles in the bedchamber. And that you would be naked. We both agreed on that."

"Even when it's freezing?"

He shook his head stood up and dropped her onto the mattress, which dipped as she bounced gently. "It's nowhere near freezing. But if you're cold you may slip under the covers. I'll join you in a moment."

"Not until you tell me who you are, you won't. I don't sleep with anyone I don't know." She crossed her arms and stared defiantly at him. "Spill the beans. You, me, where, how, why?"

There she went with incomprehensible utterances again.

"Victoria. Your name is Victoria."

She tutted. "Duh, I know that, though everyone but everyone calls me Vicky or Vic. If as I said they like their face the way it is. Who are you? Gah, I'm sounding like a stuck record."

"Christopher, known as Kit, Lord Capel, the Duke of Aulban." He paused to see if there was a glimmer of comprehension on her face.

There wasn't.

He sighed and ran his fingers through his hair.

"Your husband."

His wife stared at him, and then began to laugh.

The laugh got louder, shriller, and became hysterical.

"Now I know you're delusional." She shook her head and her long brunette curls spun around her face like a whirling, dancing mass. "I don't have a husband."

Could his day get any worse?
****

Daniel paused mid swatting the delectable arse in front of him to rub, what must be a considerable ache by now, away. His quarry had stopped screaming for this Vicky, at last, and unless his senses were completely off, she was starting to enjoy his attention. Certainly her breaths were coming in short gasps, and instead of struggling, she was raising her bottom into every carefully placed swat of his hand.

The evening was definitely looking up. As was his cock, which was in danger of splitting his evening breeches.

There was one way to find out for sure. Daniel slipped his fingers under the hideous undergarments, and smirked at the all over body shiver his girl gave. Satisfied with not only her reaction but also by the wet, hair-free cunt he found, he let his digits linger.

"Oh, god."

Her breathless moan spurred him on, and he grinned when he found her hidden pearl. She shivered again when he circled the tight nub, and Daniel set up lazy circles, designed to drive any woman wild. This chit proved no exception. The air grew heavy with the musk of aroused woman, and Daniel inhaled deeply, before he stopped the movement.

A strangled groan escaped his girl, and he tapped her arse again, when she tried to rub her cunt on his fingers.

"Oh, no, you don't. I want the truth, starting with your name, and maybe then I'll let you find release. Only on my say so, though, are we clear here, girl?"

"Fuck, yes … ow."

Her arse cheeks wobbled most satisfactorily, when he yanked that odd fabric down to her knees, and delivered a few more swats to her delectable arse. The woman had a derriere made for fucking, hips to grab onto while he sunk his cock into her body and claimed what was his. That thought made his head come up. *His*? He had no business having proprietary thoughts toward a servant like that.

"Fuck, we most certainly will, but not without you telling me who you are, so…" He delivered another open handed swat across both of her arse cheeks this time, and her answering deep throated moan made him go so hard it was a wonder he hadn't spilled in his breeches yet.

"Clara, Sir. My name is Clara."

Daniel slid his fingers through her sodden slit, and flicked her nub once, causing her to give another one of those cock hardening moans.

"Very nice, but the correct address would be my lord, chit, would it not?"

A strangled groan was his response this time, and when he withdrew his fingers again, she slumped.

"Sorry, *My Lord.*"

The girl, Clara, he mentally amended, had fire, that was for sure, if the intonation she gave his title was anything to go by. A certain amount of boldness was something Daniel certainly appreciated in his bed partners. If Clara was a lady's maid, she was wasted in that position. As his mistress, however... His mood improved dramatically as that thought took hold.

It was Christmas, time to be charitable and all that went with such bounty, and what could be better than elevating this lovely creature from her status of mere servant to his mistress.

Mind thus made up, it was time to taste her nectar and to see if what he was suspecting would be true. That Clara and he would mesh perfectly in the bedroom, and he could let his darker desires shine through.

He indulged himself by sliding several digits through her wet cunt, lubricating them with her juices, before he slipped one finger into her tight channel, and brought his thumb to press against the puckered hole, guarding that entrance.

Clara stiffened slightly, but she didn't voice any protest, and when he started to thrust the finger in her cunt slowly in and out of her, she gasped. Her hips rose in involuntary jerks, which told him how close she already was to exploding under his ministrations. Her untutored responses made him want to hurry this along, but Daniel was never an inconsiderate lover. He would give her several releases before he claimed his own.

"Good girl, and who do you work for?"

Clara moaned and writhed against him, her internal muscles fluttering around his fingers in rippling moves, which signaled her impending orgasm as clearly as the rosy flush spreading across her skin. So beautifully responsive. She jerked when he tapped her nub, and then withdrew his hand.

"Faversham Estate. Oh god, please, My Lord … I." The rest of her pretty little plea was lost in a screech as he swung her off his lap and onto his bed. Her breasts bounced most satisfactorily, and her lovely almond shaped green eyes widened further when he crawled onto the bed with her, and straddled her midriff. Daniel grasped her arms and brought them high above her head. The action made her breasts rise up in silent offering, and Daniel smirked.

"Hmm, that would mean you work for me. How delightful. Whatever position you hold here, I much prefer you in this one, unable to move and at my mercy. I'm going to tie your wrists together and tether you to one of the posts, sweet Clara. Is that acceptable to you?"

Her breathing hitched and her pupils dilated to such a degree that only a small area of moss like color remained around the outer ring. Her breasts quivered with the force of her breathing, and the scent of her nectar increased. No doubt she would be leaving a wet spot on his covers by now, and wasn't that a delightful thought.

He still needed to hear her say the words, though. His employee she might be, but he would not force his attentions where they weren't wanted. Not that it had ever been a problem. As the heir apparent to Faversham Estate, and the Duke of Hockwell, he was one of the most eligible bachelors of the ton, and well used to ducking meddling mamas and enticing widows, alike, bent on leg shackling him.

If and when he selected a bride it would be someone of his choosing and more than willing and able to accommodate his somewhat unusual needs.

Not for the first time, Daniel mused how lucky it was that both he and his cousin had similar tastes and were able to confide in each other. Not only that, at times they had worked together to ensure they had all they wanted.

"I asked you a question, girl."

"Yes, My Lord, but…"

An unwanted and surprising wave of affection gripped him when he looked down to see Clara bite her lip, and blush crimson. It was endearing the way she wore her feelings on her sleeve, and a refreshing change from the artifice of the usual women in his acquaintance.

Transferring both her wrists into one of his large hands he reached across to the nightstand to retrieve his cravat. He had to grin at the way her eyes followed his every movement, and a little whimper escaped her throat when he ran the ends of the silken material across her nipples in slow circles.

"You have an objection, my dear?" he asked, and she shook her head.

"Not exactly, but don't I get a safeword or something? At least that what happens in the books, and—" She slammed her lips shut and looked anywhere but him, when Daniel burst out laughing.

"Books, you say? I shall have to read these books you refer to. No young lady, servant or not, ought to be reading books like that." He reined in his amusement when she frowned at him. Fire flashed in her expressive eyes, and he dipped his head.

"Forgive me. I do not know what you mean by such a word, but I assume it to mean you want to use a word that makes you feel safe?"

At her nod, he dropped a kiss on her nose which made her go a little cross eyed, and made his chest feel tight. What was it about this chit that drew him like a beacon, and made him act quite so out of character? It wasn't just her looks, though had she been a lady of the ton, those alone, coupled with her fabulous curves would have drawn his attention like bee to the honey. Except the freckles!

Something else was at play here. Something indecipherable, which tugged at his heartstrings and made him want to protect her.

"Yes, because I've never done this before."

Her whispered confession should have been the equivalent of a cold dousing of water straight from the well. Daniel wasn't in the habit of deflowering virgins. They tended to get over emotional, and doing so to a member of the ton was unpardonable. He had no wish to get snared into marriage like that, and a fair few had tried in the past. It had made him even more cynical of the fairer sex and their machinations on the whole.

Delivered in Clara's throaty whisper however, the confession—one that she hadn't needed to make after all—made his prick jerk against his restraints. Daniel released his hold on Clara's wrists, lest he hurt her in his agitation, and getting off her, swung his legs over the side of the bed to give himself some breathing space.

Just to be clear he had heard her right, he had to ask.

"Never as in never having been tied up, or never as in you're *virgo intacta?*"

He inwardly grimaced at the haughty way in which those words came out of his throat, which seemed clogged with emotion. Kit would have a right laugh at him if he saw him now, that's for sure. A ripe, wet woman at his disposal and he couldn't even bring himself to look at her.

The bedcovers rustled as though she had moved, and seconds later tentative fingertips brushed over his shoulders. Innocent as the contact was it nonetheless shot darts of awareness of the woman behind him straight to his cock, and he groaned under his breath.

"The latter," she said, and Daniel shook his head, and bounded off the bed and out of her reach.

"I see." Clara frowned at him, as he dropped his voice on purpose to test her reaction. "So that was your plan, was it? Sneak up and get yourself deflowered by a duke, and then what... Cry rape? Get me to marry you, what? It won't work, you know."

Daniel knew he was being the biggest cad imaginable right now, but he had to be sure.

The most un-lady like string of inventive swear words that came out Clara's mouth were as unexpected as they were delightful.

They were followed by a barrage of cushions, one of which hit him straight in the face, "Marry you? Who on earth do you think you are? This is the twenty first century you bloody fool, not..."

Daniel didn't hear the rest of the shouted words, as the ground shook with another almighty flash of thunder and lightning. The candles went out, and the room filled with enough light to blind a man.

What in deuce was going on?

Chapter Four

Faversham House, December 1815

"Contrary to what you assume, my dear, you do have a spouse. To wit, me." That hallucination of a drop dead gorgeous bloke folded his arms, to all intents and purposes a man without a care in the world, except to hear what she had to say. She'd tell him.

"Hold on. Humor me please." Vicky wriggled until she was almost flat on the bed with only her head propped on the covers. He followed her actions with narrowed eyes but didn't speak. "Shut up and listen up."

Vicky gathered her thoughts as the feather mattress cocooned her. The sheer comfort was enough to make her want to sigh in contentment. If she hadn't been so determined to get to the bottom of what was going on, she'd have said sod it and enjoyed a nap. However.

"Right, I might sound like a tape on loop, not that I'd even know how to do that let alone get hold of one." *Shut up Vic you sound like a moron.*

He frowned.

"Yes I'm babbling again, sorry. Right." She forced her shoulders down and tried to relax. It was hard when she was so churned up. "Please just tell me what happened to get me tied down, naked, in your bed. Straightforward and with no embellishments."

He did that one raised eyebrow thing that sent her pussy into spasms. Bloody hell, at this rate the sheet would be two toned and she'd be damp and uncomfortable.

Damn him.

"Our bed, and sadly, not what would usually

happens when you're fastened, naked there."

That sentence spoken in *that* voice was hard not to respond to by a fast move from the bed, onto the floor and on her knees in front of him.

She also could do the one eyebrow thing, sadly not with as much style and panache as the man who now very slowly unwrapped his yard long cravat from his neck and ran it through his fingers. Her gesture seemed lost on him as he held the cravat in the air and chuckled. "This would usually be used somehow. When allowed, you can be most inventive."

Allowed? Vicky decided that if she wanted to ever find out what was going on she'd better let that outrageous comment pass unremarked.

He put the cravat onto the back of a chair and turned to the cuffs of his shirt. It looked as if she might be about to see the guy in a much more natural light. Would it be cool to punch the air and shout yee haa?

Maybe not.

Instead she waited until he'd pulled the shirt over his head and prompted him. "So?"

So." He wandered, bare-chested, over to one corner of the room and used a bootjack to pull off his gleaming hessians. The firelight emphasized the play of his muscles as he moved and the tight breeches showed his buttocks off to perfection.

Vicky watched him, dry mouthed as he bent over to stand his boots outside the door, and turned back to look at her as he closed the door and locked it.

"We don't need servants interrupting us."

Well, no, but who on earth were the servants? As far as Vicky knew only Clara and the caretaker husband and wife team were permanent staff and no way were they classified as servants.

The guy ... her husband—allegedly—walked

back to the bed and sat on the edge. She looked pointedly at his groin where his cock was outlined long and hard under the creamy-colored material that hid it from view. He followed her gaze and smiled ruefully.

"A permanent state of affairs around you, my heart."

"Maybe it needs air? You know instead of being confined under those." She waved her hand in the direction of his prick. "I don't mind."

He laughed. "Nor would my pego."

Pego? I thought that was only used in books. I use it in mine, but by god he's taking this dress in Regency costumes a bit too far isn't he? Talking in it as well. Ah well as long as I find out what's going on and where Clo… hell, I'd forgotten Clara.

"Clara?" she blurted out. "Is she okay?"

He stayed his fingers as they opened the placket on his breeches and blinked. "Who?"

"The girl I was with and… oh look just tell me everything, then you can answer my questions."

"*Ma petite.*"

The warning tone in his voice made her shiver with an *ohh what next* thought. However…

"Look, sorry or whatever but I'm sort of worried here," she said placatingly. A thought struck her. "Do you know where my ba…reticule is." At least she could use the correct name for the pretty drawstring bag that matched the dress she'd worn.

He bent down to the base of the cabinet by the bed. The one she thought might contain a commode. It didn't, but that thought made her want to use one.

As he straightened and handed her the reticule Vicky wondered just what was more important. Finding out what was happening, going to the bathroom, or checking the contents of her bag were still intact. Her bladder decided for her.

"Um where's the loo please?" At his blank look she mentally rolled her eyes. *Asshole.*

"Excuse me, I need the…" The what? "The facilities," she finished finally. "The withdrawing room." Her skin heated and she wanted to slide under the covers. Why was it that to ask where the loo was didn't faze her but asking in such an antiquated manner made her blush?

He pointed to one side of the room. Only the twinkle in his eyes showed how amused he was by her reaction. "Through that door. Where there is also a bath, and a ewer and warm water. I hesitate to say it's hot as I brought it up earlier, but at least it won't be freezing."

Vicky nodded. "Thank you." Now if only she had something to wrap herself in. His expression showed her he damn well knew what was going through her mind and expected her to ask for a robe. Well, sod it, she went naked at home, she could do it here. She'd just ignore him.

That of course was easier said than done.

With an insouciance she certainly didn't feel, Vicky threw the cover back and stood up. He, damn him, didn't take his eyes off her. Now she knew how a bug pinned out for inspection felt.

He grinned and flicked his finger over her denuded pussy.

"Nice to see your cunt without a covering of hair."

"Too personal, mate." Vicky turned her back on him. "Watch it."

The swat to her ass was unexpected and stung. She swung round again. "What the fuck was that for?"

"Brass is not accepted."

Vicky thought fast. She thought he'd used brass to mean impudence not outrageous.

"You mean I'm bratty? I know that. Sass is my middle name."

"No, your middle name is Sarah."

****

Kit watched as she wrinkled her nose. He had no idea what bratty or sass meant but he'd guess she meant she answered a question with another and took nothing for granted without querying it first. If that was, what did she say, sass, he liked it.

"Sarah?" she said finally. "How do you know that?"

"Wedding vows. I, Victoria Sarah do marry, and so on."

"Yeah, well about that marriage malarkey … hold on, look I really do need to go." She turned on her heel and left the room at a run.

Kit watched and knew he had a smile on his face. His Victoria might have woken up with some strange ideas in her head but she still did everything at top speed. He stripped his stockings and breeches down his legs and, as naked as she, stretched out on the bed. Used to the temperature he didn't bother going under the covers. It might be only a little above the temperature needed to put ice on his drinking water, but it didn't bother him or his cock. He was pleasantly warm and his cock, heated by their exchange, was as stiff as it ever became.

Kit counted three minutes in his head before the door opened and his wife returned. He looked her up and down, as ever admiring her racehorse sleek body. She glowered.

"Stop that. I know it's all a sham. I'm not well endowed and I look like a boy."

What? "If you think that, you need to be put over my knee. Does this," he ran his hand over his cock from base to tip, collected the juices that had already gathered and held it toward her, "give you that impression? I'm not interested in boys. I never was, not even at Eton. Taste," he commanded. "Come here and taste what just looking at you does to me."

Would she? Kit had no illusions that if she chose not to, he wouldn't chastise her. Any spanking or flogging was consensual and within the remit of their dynamique. As young men, one stormy night, he and his cousin had emptied several bottles of his Papa's best— and smuggled—brandy, and swapped sexual encounters and preferences. To both their pleasure and amazement, they'd discovered they each had a penchant for things not usually discussed between the gentlemen of the ton, and certainly not admitted to being part of a man's usual proclivities. Partly, he assumed because few women would let such things happen. To indulge in bondage or flogging one had to employ the services of a courtesan or demi-monde. To discover that when, by accident he flicked his riding crop over his wife's rear she'd moaned in ecstasy, had been an eye opener. To hear her admission that she liked it, and was ready to try other things he enjoyed, had set the seal on their successful marriage.

He would do nothing to lose that rapport.

"*Ma petite.*" His hope, that by using her name for their play, she'd obey, was realized. Victoria swallowed deeply and walked toward him, dipped her head, and sucked his finger deep into her mouth. She looked up at him from under lowered lashes. "You taste magnificent, but…"

He seized the advantage. "Oh your knees over me, and suck me until my juices fill your mouth."

She moved and climbed over him. Her pert breasts were at eye level and he took hold of her nipples and squeezed. Her hiss of indrawn breath was all he could ask for.

"Down on me." He understood how his terse uttered commands made her wet. With a bare cunt he could see her skin glisten with her juices and watch as her nether lips became red and engorged. Next he knew she'd try to rub herself over him, make enticing little erotic mewls and do her best to gain her release. Not yet.

"Do not touch yourself in any way. Make me spill, then we'll see." He tweaked her nipples one last time and leaned back once more. "Eat me, *ma petite.*"

She stroked his cock from tip to base with her tongue and circled his girth, before she tightened her mouth round him and began to suck and release. Up and down, slowly and faster. Her fingers found his bollocks and fondled and squeezed them, just as he liked.

Kit's breath grew labored and harsh. "Hell, yes, more faster, oh sweet lord. Yes..." He saw stars as she thrust the tip of her tongue into the slit of his cock and nipped the sensitive head with her teeth.

His seed spurted out of him as she swallowed and sucked him ever faster. Kit shook, gripped her head and surrendered to the sweetest sensation ever.

Several minutes later, Kit stared at the woman, who stirred by his side, rolled onto her front, knelt up, stretched her arms high in the air and smiled down at him.

"Mm...mmmm." She grinned. "Got to say I enjoyed that."

My wife, my love, my life. Six words to fill him with satisfaction.

"Your turn, *ma petite*. Now what first, I wonder? Do I tie you, flog you and fuck your darkness? Or fill you with my seed and wonder if we create our first child."

"You er ... what?" Her eyes widened, she blinked

and gasped. "Oh shit what have I done?"

Why was she talking about bodily functions in such a manner? And she seemed perturbed, not at all as she normally would when he made such suggestions.

Kit opened his mouth to ask what she meant when she scrambled over him, nearly de-balling him in her haste. His cock must have seen near disaster because it deflated the fastest he had ever known. If it could, Kit would swear it wouldn't have stopped at slinking between his legs but snuck behind his ass instead.

He let his breath out in one long whoosh when she stood next to the bed and frantically looked around.

"Definitely both. On your knees, head on the pillow."

"Yeah, yeah, hold on a sec." It was obvious she hadn't listened to him. "Where's that sodding bag? Ha, thank the lord." She ignored Kit as she lifted the reticule she had grabbed and upended the contents on the covers next to him.

Kit stared. What on earth had she got in there? Nothing was familiar to him. Except, he saw with relief, a fan. He watched carefully as she scrabbled between strange shapes and boxes and pulled out a package, and waved it high in triumph.

"Yes! I knew I'd got some with me. We do nothing unless you jacket up." She paused and looked at him closely. "Hey, just because I carry condoms doesn't mean I'm easy or a slut, okay? I'm open and honest and don't agree to a double standard. If a guy can say he wants to shag, why shouldn't a woman? Likewise I carry condoms, tampons—cos lord I'm about as regular as a London bus—along with a spare pair of contacts, wet wipes, and make sure my safety buddy knows where I am. Which reminds me, where am I exactly?" She picked up a small shiny oblong box and looked at him expectantly. "Then, once I've let Clo know where you've got me, we can…" She blushed. His confusion must have shown on his face. Lord, his wife did talk in riddles some times. Had she always been as bad?

Yes.

"Oh hell, you hate it don't you?" She sighed dramatically. "You want a simpering milksop, not an in-your-face stroppy cow. If you show me where my dress is, I'll leave you to it."

He stopped her rapid shuffle by the simple expedient of grabbing her by the elbow and holding tight. "You, *ma petite*," Kit said evenly, "are talking in riddles. Why would I suddenly take an aversion to my wife? The wife I married, knowing full well how assertive she could be, as well as how submissive. The wife I want and love with every fiber of my being. The wife whom I worship. The wife who completes me and makes me whole." He twitched her over his knee before he hoped she had a chance to assimilate what he intended. "The wife who infuriates me, fucks me senseless, and tells me how much she loves me as often as I tell her I love her. All the time. The wife to whom this is a much longed for caress." He swatted each round globe of her arse several times and rejoiced in her long drawn out "ohhh, yesss."

"The wife whose ideas mesh with mine and loves the sweet sting of my hand on her rear as much as I love giving it to her." He rubbed the redness he had inflicted. "More?"

"Oh yes … oh shit, please, please make me… Argh what the hell am I *saying*?" She began to struggle. "Bloody hell on wheels, let me up, now." She bucked and as her elbow hit him squarely in the bollocks he wheezed and let her flip off his lap to stand in front of him, arms akimbo.

"You've addled my brains. What a load of tripe

you're spouting. I'm single. I'm Lady Victoria Hopewell. I live in St John's Wood, I'm twenty-five, and I write Regency novels for a living."

"No." He spoke slowly and kept a wary eye on her hands and how close she was to anything throwable. If she got her dander up and became roiled, he needed to know there was nothing valuable or heavy within her reach. "You were Lady Victoria Hopewell but upon our marriage you became my duchess."

"So you say. When, pray, were we married?" Skeptical was an understatement. Mistrust oozed out of her.

"Almost twelve months ago." Kit kept his voice flat and unemotional. He daren't show how much this interchange affected him. "On Christmas Eve."

"Hmm." She began to pace fast, striding from one side of the room to the other. "Tell me more and fast."

Lord, he'd soon be dizzy if he watched her for long. Dare he ask her to stop pacing and calm down? One swift glance at her stormy countenance decided that. Not if he valued his bollocks.

"What do you want to know?" How on earth could he convince his wife she *was* his wife? That they did live in Regency times and as yet were not blessed with a child but he intended to remedy that soon?

"That would be what year?" Victoria demanded. "When you say we tied the knot."

"1814."

"No shit, Sherlock. It can't have been."

"As today is December 1815, so it follows that this time last year was December 1814."

"Oh hell in a hand basket." She sat down heavily and began to turn that strange oblong box over and over in her hands. Once she did something to it, held it to her ear and then dropped it onto the bed beside her with a grunt of disgust. "Dead as a dodo. Figures. Look, are you sure?"

Why was she so insistent on him repeating the date to her? Surely she knew what day it was? "When we worried about our world and what would become of it? I'm sure. Even though Bonaparte was imprisoned, those in the know were concerned about his plans and his growing army of supporters. With good reason it turned out. Anyway, that apart, we chose the eve of Christ's birth to, well, to start the birth of something new and good. Our marriage."

"Where? Where did we do it?"

He jumped. That was a singularly stupid question. "Here, of course, in the chapel." Where else would a duke wed? "We were going to go to our house in the woods to celebrate."

She looked at him blankly. Kit made haste to explain. "The one where we play whenever we can. My betrothal present to you, for us." She still stared at him with no comprehension showing on her face. Kit sighed. "A small house near the west wood, equipped for us by us and where no servants are allowed. Mainly because what we get up to there might get me hanged, and you exiled. However, nature foiled our plans. There was a tremendous storm, similar to the one tonight and so we began our married life here, in this room." He grinned. "We can both be very inventive when need be. You did say you'd never look upon the curtain ties in the same way ever again." He paused and winked. "I offered to have them framed."

Chapter Five

Faversham House, December 2015

Clara blinked in the sudden light, and breathed a sigh of relief at the welcome return of electricity. The old-fashioned radiators, which she so admired, whirred into action with their usual clanking sounds. The half-naked man in front of her spun around as though he was expecting to find a masked intruder in his bedroom. Muscles bunched and released in his back when he bent down to pick up a wicked looking hunting knife off the oriental rug that covered the wooden flooring in front of the huge four poster bed she was sitting on… *naked… Oh, god I'm naked in front of a complete stranger, who will see everything if he turns around. One I almost had sex with.*

Clara barely suppressed a shriek at her thought processes. Reality set in with a vengeance. None of this had been a dream. With the perfect replica of a Regency bed chamber bathed in light, this man—whose tight ass she couldn't help but admire as the soft material of his breeches hugged his behind—this hunk, who would put Raven McAllan's Jack Trevithan to shame—would be able to see every last one of her wobbly bits. Not that she was ashamed of her body, far from it, and at least in her favorite Regency erotica writer's books, the men of those times always enjoyed their ladies' soft curves, but this wasn't a book on her Kindle. This was her life, and she had the throbbing pussy and smarting ass cheeks to remind her of that.

"What sort of magic is this?" His deep voice took on that gravelly note of annoyance that seemed to be a livewire to her libido. Just like she had done when she'd been draped over his knees, her pussy muscles spasmed, and the top of her thighs grew wet with her arousal. She'd been on the verge of coming earlier, and it wouldn't take much to send her over the edge now.

"Kit, is that you? Enough, you had your fun. This stops now. I know you must be hiding somewhere." He looked round the room as though searching for something, and when he turned back in her direction Clara made a hasty grab for the first thing she could find to cover her nakedness, which happened to be the shirt he'd been wearing. Once she had pushed her head through the opening, and fumbled with the strings she was somewhat covered, if you ignored her boobs playing peekaboo through the gap. His gaze snared on her assets briefly, and a secret thrill went through her system, when he groaned and adjusted his cock. The action made her look at his groin, and her throat went dry at the long, thick imprint lovingly outlined by his breeches. There was something to be said for men's Regency wear when you looked as buff as this guy. What had he said his name was again? Daniel, something. Duke of Hockwell, that was it. That name rang a distant bell in her befuddled brain.

How did you address a duke again? "Hockwell."

He frowned at her shout, yanked his gaze upward to her face, and her heart missed a beat at the confusion she read in his ice blue eyes.

"That's My Lord to you, chit. This whole façade ends now. You and my cousin had your fun at my expense. I bet your name isn't even Clara, and you're no lady's maid. More an accomplished actress from Drury Lane. Damn you, Kit, where are you?"

Ignoring Clara's shake of her head, he stormed past the bed and opened the door on the other side of this chamber.

"Deuce, that's…"

More light flooded into the room, as the light in the ultra-modern wet room came on automatically, and the fan clicked on. Daniel sagged against the wall, and turned so white, Clara was half expecting him to pass out.

He'd accused her of being an actress, yet he must be giving the performance of his life. Who would play such a prank on her though? Certainly not the stoic James, and Vicky… No, as outspoken and fun loving as her newfound friend was, she took her research into Regency times and in particular the missing heir far too seriously. No wonder her books were so popular. When Clara had been told that Lady Victoria Hopewell—one of her favorite Regency romance authors—was going to shadow her for a few weeks and learn all about the house, the family and the missing heir, she'd been over the moon.

The missing heir… *No, it can't be.*

Not for the first time that evening Clara cursed the amount of drink she'd consumed. It still made her brain feel stuffed with wool, and no doubt was the main reason why she'd come close to losing her virginity in the dark to this man. She could almost imagine the pulse between her legs strum in tune to the reckless part of her brain wishing they hadn't stopped when they did. Sadly, Daniel looked as far removed from being in the mood for a good fuck as it was possible to be. She noticed with grim amusement that his erection had deflated considerably.

"Daniel, I'm not." His head shot up and the flash of some undefined deep emotion she glimpsed in his gaze took her breath away, and made her heart miss a beat. Fleeting as that moment of connection was, she still felt it all the way to her toes.

"What year do you think this is?" she asked abruptly.

He blinked, and straightening, frowned into the wet room again.

"1815, of course." His eyes drew together and when the full force of his azure gaze settled on her, Clara didn't dare move. Breathing proved difficult and her pussy muscles started up their *take me, I'm yours* dance again. It was beyond ridiculous the effect he had on her with just one glance, but she couldn't deny the connection arching between them like a living entity. With it came the certain knowledge that this man was important to her, that he was the one man she had been subconsciously waiting for all this time. After all, her beloved grandmother had always said, she would know him.

"One glance was all it took for me to know your grandfather was the one for me, and life would never be the same again." Taking her words to heart, Clara had waited for that moment, and, in truth, had all but given up on it ever happening, which was fine. She had her work and her naughty books, after all. Until this Regency duke literally appeared in front of her.

Oh god, the storm, him appearing. Time travel, is that my reality now?

"I suppose you are going to tell me the year is something ridiculous like 3003." Daniel's deep voice mocked her, and pulled her out of her internal thoughts. He seemed to have recovered some of his equilibrium, if the haughty way he looked down his aristocratic nose at her was anything to go by. And that should make him a complete and utter asshole, not hotter than hell, surely.

"No that would be ridiculous. The year is 2015, *My Lord.*"

His eyes flashed fire at her, and she swallowed hard when he pushed away from the wall and advanced toward her. Like the prey caught in the headlights of impending disaster, she couldn't move, just sat there, all too aware of how little she wore, and the fact that her nipples were doing their best to stick out and wave at him like the *checkered flag* at the race course.

"And that is not ridiculous, I suppose." He stopped just in front of the bed, and towered over her. A tall, somewhat menacing presence.

"Not to me, it isn't." Her voice came out somewhat wobbly, but there, she'd said it.

"Then prove it to me."

Clara knew her mouth fell open at that imperious command, and the smirk that pulled his lips up sealed the deal.

Ignoring her body's almost overwhelming urge to sink to her knees in front of him, and to beg him to finish what they'd started, she squared her shoulders, and got off the bed on the other side with as much dignity as she could, which wasn't much at all.

"Fine, I will, let me just find my bag… ah here it is." Clara spotted the tiny drawstring bag which had come with her costume. She didn't need the sudden draft up her backside to know that she had just flashed her whereforalls to Daniel, when she picked the thing up off the floor. His sharp intake of breath confirmed he liked what he saw, and when she spun around, mobile phone in hand, she wasn't entirely surprised to see him tenting his breeches again.

At least she wasn't the only one to feel the combustible heat between them. He frowned when she clicked it on and the display lit up. Opening up her internet browser she brought up the website for Haversham House, and with a triumphant snort shoved the phone at him.

"Here, see. That's the website for Haversham House, and that has me listed as the curator, and James and Brenda, as permanent caretakers."

"Impossible." He sat down with a thump, and she gentled her voice as she guided his fingers across the screen. His breathing sped up and his knuckles turned white in the strangle hold he had on her phone, as she took him through the site.

"And you see, here on the blog is the invite to the Regency Christmas Ball. We do this every year in an effort to find the heir, he…"

His head came up at the mention of an heir, and the fine hair on her arms rose at his murmured response.

"Through time and space…you don't belong…hell and tarnation."

He got up so abruptly, she almost fell off the bed. Not that Daniel noticed because he paced up and down the length of the room like a caged tiger, and then almost yanked the bell pull off its mooring.

"Erm, you're not expecting that to work, do you, because…" She stopped speaking at his incredulous look, and held up her phone. "Let me text him. Cause they're just decoration … I think anyway."

"You think? You're the curator, and you think? Surely you would know what you've done with my house?"

****

His cock tightened seeing Clara's reaction to his words. She looked thoroughly roiled at him questioning her abilities, and he hid his smirk when she got to her knees and, hand on hips, glared at him. If looks could kill, he would have already met his maker, and he wasn't entirely sure this whole episode wasn't a wine fueled hallucination on his part. After all, he'd grown beyond wary at the machinations of his time, and the expectancy of the ton for him to settle down and marry, when nobody suitable for his needs had presented themselves. Daniel had always known he would never settle for anything but true love in a marriage and seeing Kit so much in love with his Lady Victoria had only cemented that belief.

"How dare you? I'm perfectly capable of doing my job, or at least I would be, if this wing wasn't locked away and my hands weren't tied with the idiotic rules set by your ancestor, this Lord Reginald gay as a fence post Danvers, who thus died childless, and what?"

Her ire increased in tune to his amusement, and he grew even harder. Damn it all, he would have to have her and soon, or explode. All this talking, as important as it was, was getting them nowhere fast, and he wanted, no needed to lose himself in her sweet body.

Knelt on the bed as she was with the light of the oil lamp right behind her, his shirt was rendered transparent, and all her lush curves were on display, which made his cock behave like a champion race horse galloping toward the finishing line.

"What's so freaking funny about that?"

Daniel reigned in his merriment with some difficulty.

"I could ask you the same question. What has this Reginald being a very happy man have to do with him not leaving an heir? Dashed inconsiderate as that was of him."

Clara harrumphed, that was really the only word for it, and rolled her eyes.

"Oh, for pity's sake, he was gay as in homosexual, batting for the other team, and all that, jazz, not that there is anything wrong with being gay. Love is love after all, but you know, it doesn't render itself to providing precious heirs."

Daniel had no idea what she was talking about. She might as well be speaking another language.

"He wasn't able to perform?" he guessed.

Clara snorted. It should have been an incongruous sound but coupled with her wrinkling her nose, it was strangely erotic.

"I wasn't there, so I couldn't possibly answer that, but it was more a case of he couldn't get it up for women, if you catch my drift."

Daniel had no idea what snowdrifts had to do with anything, but he thought it wisest to keep that thought to himself. Really this woman had some strange sayings and even stranger beliefs. Suddenly her words registered with him.

"You mean he preferred the company of men." At Clara's nod, he shrugged his shoulders and grinned. "That is not entirely surprising. A fair number of men in my family seem to be that way inclined. Even so, he should have put his personal preferences aside long enough to maintain his duty, and provided an heir to the estate."

A discreet cough behind him alerted Daniel to the fact that they weren't alone anymore. Clara shrieked and, grabbing hold of the bed curtain, used it to shield her half naked state as much as she could. Why she should be that embarrassed to be caught in a state of undress in front of a servant was beyond Daniel's comprehension. His own valet had seen him in all sorts of state of undress and compromising situations and never batted an eyelid, but the silver haired man dressed in full Regency butler attire wasn't Jenkins of course. No, this was the man in the picture on the strange little black box Clara had shown him. Dressed as he was in full Regency attire, the likeness of this man to the butler of Faversham house in

1815 was startling to the extreme.

This butler bowed his head, and with a hint of amusement in his grey eyes, smiled toward Clara hiding on the bed before he sobered and addressed Daniel.

"My lord, if I may be so bold as to offer an opinion to this dilemma?"

Behind him Clara snorted again, and Daniel was sure he heard her mutter some sort of expletive that would have made sailors blush in his time.

"By all means do, if you know something to shed some insight into this dilemma as you put it."

James smiled again, and took a folded parchment out of the inside of his suit. Daniel's heart beat faster when he recognized Kit's seal on the back of the aged paper.

"Lord Danvers did leave an heir. You, my lord."

Chapter Six

Haversham House, December 1815

Vicky wondered if she'd wake up any time soon. She clutched her dead as a dodo phone and stared at the condoms and the rest of the paraphernalia spread out around her. She had to be dreaming. Researching for a book sometimes did that to her. She seemed to remember a storm and a wedding. Of marrying a drop dead gorgeous guy who liked the same things as she did. Hell, she'd almost finished plotting the book. The only part of it she didn't know was how it was going to end. Maybe this dream would show her?

"And tonight?" she asked and cursed the apprehension that made her voice wobble.

Kit gave her a shrewd look, took a deep breath and began to talk.

Ten minutes later she had an incipient headache and her eyes were gritty. Come what may, she'd have to take her lenses out soon, and put on her specs. Would that freak him out? Somehow she doubted it. So far nothing she'd said or done had upset his even tone and his level attitude towards her and her stroppiness. Because, she was uneasily aware, stroppy was an understatement. But hey, surely she had good reason to be a bit bratty.

"I'm sorry if I've riled you," she began. "But ya know it's a bit much to take in without a hangover."

"Riled? Do you mean roiled?"

She shrugged. "Probably, whatever I apologize. It's a lot to assimilate." Somehow she'd have to bite her tongue, eat humble pie, and accept any punishment her

Lord and master thought fit. Vicky acknowledged she deserved it. "However I'll do my best. So, let me get this straight." Not that she had any idea how. "I'm your wife, it's 1815, and we were at a ball?"

He nodded. "The annual estate ball. We were in the picture gallery."

"So why was I naked?"

He blinked. "Ah. You like being naked? It's what we decided on."

"Not good enough," Vicky said, even though those words in his deep commanding tone made her pussy sting and goose bumps skitter over her skin. She tried to ignore how she felt and concentrated on what she needed to know. "I surely wasn't naked at a ball?" That could have come from one of her novels. The one where the heroine had a dream and woke up in… *Oh shit … I'm living my book.* "Tell me I wasn't."

He laughed. "No, that was after you screamed the place down when the storm was overhead. You were sweating so much I stripped you to towel you down. Then, well, you know the rest."

Do I? Maybe, maybe not.

"We were at a ball in when, 2015?"

He put his hand to her forehead. "You don't feel feverish."

"I'm not. I'm not feverish, delusional or a crackpot. I don't think." To be honest she wasn't sure anymore. "But will you cuddle me anyway?" More and more Vicky thought that, crazy or not, this guy loomed large and was important in her life. She'd always had premonitions and this one became ever more fixed in her mind. Why else did she know so much about the era without research? Why was she such a stickler for detail? Maybe there was something in this time travel thing after all. Either that or the mushroom quiche she'd had at lunch was suspect.

"Okay, just for supposition's sake, let's say it is 1815, and I'm married to you," she said, rapidly thinking things out as she voiced her thoughts. "We went to a ball and it thundered. I imagined it was two hundred years in the future, grabbed some things and now we're back in your—our time. I know what I brought back and you have no idea what they're for. Have I got that right?"

He nodded. "Essentially, yes. Except I joined you after you'd gone."

"Okay so to go on from there. How did I get into 2015 anyway, and how come you were with me?" She was half talking to herself but he heard her, because he grunted in what? Agreement? Dissent? She didn't ask. "Why didn't you hold on to me when I... well whatever I—we—did to get there? And how come I've got my lenses and stuff with me? How did I know what to get?" She pointed at him and poked him in the stomach. "Ha, you don't have an answer, do you?" she finished triumphantly.

He took hold of her hand and bit the flesh part of skin just above her thumb. Vicky gasped. "What the?" *Oh my.* That sweet sting was too much sensory overload for her at that moment. She had enough to assimilate with the fact her life could well not be what she thought it was, without a pussy going into overdrive and a need for some lady pads. Did they even have anything vaguely like them in Regency times? The most she'd ever found in her research was sponges and vinegar for birth control and one very discrete paragraph about a wad of linen inserted inside as, she guessed, a very rudimentary tampon for that time of the month. Was that to be her life from now on?

"You talk too much," Kit said. Funny how now his name came into her mind naturally. "And what you said? Well a lot of that doesn't make sense, *ma petite.* Earlier today you went out on your horse. A storm got up and you were thrown. You only lost consciousness for a short while, and seemed fine. We went to the estate ball." His diction was clipped and terse. "Entered the picture gallery and you changed in front of my eyes." He gulped, so unlike his normal self that Vicky gaped at him in amazement. Her next thought hit her like a ton of bricks.

Hold on, how do I know what his normal self is like? This is shit stirringly scary. "Um, in what way changed?"

He shrugged. "It's hard to say. You just left me for a while. Then, well, we had more thunder, you screamed, grabbed hold of me, and I dragged you out of the gallery and into here. Back to our room where I held you, and you know the rest."

Well, actually, no she didn't, but one thing seemed to be clear. It *was* 1815, she *was* married and this hunk *was* her husband.

Where was the gin when you needed it?

"Then if this is 1815, and we're married and I don't live in 2015, how do I have my contacts in, a box of condoms, a packet of tampons, and designer glasses to change into? And where is Clara?"

"Clara?"

"The curator of the house. The girl I was with when that bloke … that bloke he looked like you … who was he?"

Kit turned a nice shade of white, and mumbled something under his breath. Vicky stared at him as he swayed and visibly collected himself.

"What?" she asked urgently. "What is it? What do you know?"

"Hockwell? The tall blond man with me? He's my cousin, and tarnation. I haven't seen him since we got back. I'm certain he didn't follow us. Do you think he's gone back, forward or whatever with this Clara?"

"What do you mean?" *Gah, I'm doing the repetition crap again.*

"Well, do you recall always saying that he struck you as odd?" At her blank look he ran a hand through his hair and sighed. "Well, you did. Called it female intuition. You said, and I quote, he doesn't really seem to fit here, does he? And come to think of it, you're right. Oh, Daniel could play the game as well as the next person, but I thought it was just because of that strange prophecy he got as a child."

"Prophesy?" Vicky echoed.

"Yes, we got a royal telling off by our governesses, but we'd sneaked away to the travelling fair, and into the hut of Mistress Allure." Kit smirked as he remembered. "Her only allure consisted of having seemingly managed to have lived to one hundred, if you counted the lines on her face. Anyhow, she read us our fortune. Mine was the usual, as befitting my station. His? Well, she smiled, turned his hand over, patted his head and said 'Poor child, your place is not here. Fear not, because all will become clear when you follow your heart and cross space and time'."

Vicky was transfixed. "And you? What did she say to you?"

He went red and muttered something under his breath.

"Pardon? I didn't hear that."

He muttered again. This time Vicky caught some of the words. Mainly, *married, seven* and *offspring*. She poked him on the arm.

He winced and glared. "Violence is never the answer."

"Don't you believe it, mate. Sometimes it's the

only answer. Did you say what I think you did? That you reckon we're having seven kids? In your dreams, buster, think again. Or violence might well be the result."

"It's written," Kit said in a voice that brooked no arguments.

"Typical male. In the stars I suppose," Vicky said sarcastically. "Not a scooby. Stars, charlatans or charts, and it's written, bloody well hold no truck with me. If I write, Kit has his bollocks chopped off with a rusty pen knife would you say okay, it's written?"

He moved his hands swiftly to cover his cock and balls and Vicky nodded with satisfaction.

"Ha, exactly. Hence if you think I'm going to lie back, think of England and shell out seven kids like peas popping from a pod you've got another think coming. What do you imagine these are for?" She upended the supersized box of condoms over his head and threw the now empty box after them, followed by three tampons and, just because they were handy, her contact lens case and the wet wipes.

His eyes widened as one foil covered condom hit him on the nose, and a tampon wedged behind his ear. It looked so like a sketch in an anarchical TV program her parents had raved about, Vicky bit back a giggle.

"What in Hades, woman?" His look of rage gave her pause. Vicky took a step away from him, towards the door. "Ah... I er…" She didn't get any further. Kit pulled her back and tipped her chin up.

"What was that for?" he asked levelly. "Seven is not excessive. I need some heirs."

"Some yes." She understood that. "Surely not seven?"

"Why not?" He seemed genuinely perplexed. "You'll have help."

Everything was going much too fast. Seven was

six more than she'd ever envisaged having. Grief, she knew enough about either of her personas to know she was no earth mother.

"Well, if you use those," she waved a condom at him. "I'll have even more help. And hopefully less kids."

****

"Oufft! What the—"

"Enough." Kit tucked his wife under his arm and dropped her onto the bed before he followed her and kept her in place by the simple expediency of putting his leg over her waist. Unfortunately, at the angle he'd landed that put his cock in line with her cunt.

Down, boy, not yet. He willed his wayward pego to behave and concentrate on his wife.

Her cheeks were delicately flushed, her lips were slightly apart, and her skin slicked with the sheen of arousal. She took a deep breath and he braced himself for her ire.

It didn't come.

"You see that little thing you have in your hand?" she said quietly. "That will prevent children."

He stared at a tiny square packet made of some material he'd never seen before. Surely she jested? "How on earth?"

She stretched up and plucked it out of his fingers. As Kit watched in amazement she tugged and the packet fell to bits.

"See?" Victoria took out a tiny almost see through… see through what? and shook it. "Now you put this on and lo and behold no little wrigglies get through and think aha a nice warm womb to spend some time in. Instead they get caught up and flushed away, not to live another day."

"On where?" With a bit of luck it would cover his big toe or his thumb, but even he knew neither digit produced children.

"On your cock."

Kit narrowed his eyes. "My cock is not a bantam. That whatever it is wouldn't even cover a puppy's prick and I'm no puppy."

Victoria rolled her eyes. She was very good at conveying so many different emotions in that one small gesture. "Men and their bits. Take it from me it's guaranteed to fit. Hot dog eh? From a chipolata to a Cumberland. Okay neither of those fit the bill." She chuckled. "Well I don't think so. Argh, that sounds as if I'm dissing your attributes and I'm not. After all who wants a Cumberland in them? A long curly cock's not much good."

What on earth was she talking about? Kit decided it was high time to wrest the initiative back from her before she really confused him. He wanted to sink his cock into her, not discuss its non-human like attributes.

"My cock is happy as it is, not squeezed into, well whatever that is."

"A condom. A prophylactic, rubber, Johnny, raincoat, French letter, willy cover, whatever, take your pick. Birth control other than the slap hazard manner of pull out and shoot elsewhere."

He flicked the condom onto the floor. "I have a linen sheath, but if you remember correctly you said it was, and I quote, akin to filling you cunt with sand. Abrasive you said was an understatement and we declared it unusable. If you don't wish my seed in you, I'll withdraw and spill onto a towel." But why would he need to? They were married and he needed an heir. "However, you said you loved the feel of me filling you, coming deep inside you and making you shout out in pleasure. The heat of my seed as it gathers pace and floods you is a sensation that surpasses all others.

Therefore why deny us that?"

Victoria wriggled until his cock no longer tickled her pussy, and Kit relaxed enough to let her. He wanted her as soon as possible in all ways imaginable, but knew at this moment she needed to set the pace.

"Look, I seem to have had a weird few hours," she said slowly. "Hours? God knows. Anyway. As much as I'd like to have you in me bareback, not at this present moment in time I wouldn't. I need time to assimilate everything. So it's cover up or no nookie."

Kit found the funny side of it— after all he was to all intents and purposes in these enlightened Regency times allowed to dictate their lives and here was his wife laying down the law. Not only that, he was happy to let her. He laughed, even though he had no idea what nookie was. He could, however hazard a guess. "Who wears the breeches?"

His lovely Victoria glowered. "Literally? For the next hundred and so years you do. Metaphorically? Both of us." She wriggled and damned if his wayward cock didn't register the movement as one designed to entice him to announce his presence even more forcefully and let several drops of essence coat her tummy. "And tell that," she pointed at his pego, "to mind its own business. This is between you and me. Argh." She hit her forehead dramatically. "Grr. Now I'm giving your prick a mind of its own."

Kit grinned. "Sometimes I think it already has one."

Chapter Seven

Vicky stared at him until his lips twitched, and then began to laugh. "Now if it starts to talk back to us, we'll know we're in the twilight zone." Her laughter increased until he wondered if he'd need to slap her. Then she shuddered and swallowed several times before she wrapped her arms around herself and sighed. Perspiration dotted her skin and he was certain tears clung to her lashes. He ached to kiss them away, but forced himself to stay where he was. First things first.

"It's all true isn't it?" she asked, slowly. "It really is 1815, I really am married to you and well, I either flashed forward to the future, am a seer, or a candidate for Bedlam. I think I prefer the first."

"No Bedlam. It wouldn't do the credibility of my line any good. For the rest? Whichever way you chose to interpret it, you are my wife. Believe it, my dear."

Kit leaned forward and kissed her hard on the lips. That brief touch grounded her more than any words ever could. Somewhere deep down inside her she recognized it. Recognized him. If she were honest it scared the shit out of her.

The whole scenario did. Here she was in her mind a 21st century girl, a fully paid up member of the 'women are equal' society, accepting without an argument that no, actually that was a load of shite.

"Okay then."

He raised one sculptured eyebrow. Did they even have tweezers now … then … oh lord whenever? And would a bloke use them anyway. *Shit this back in time crap is fraught with danger.*

"Do you pluck?" she blurted out.

"Pluck?" His expression was puzzled and then it cleared. "Ah you mean fuck? Well, my dear, you should know."

Evidently no he didn't. Okay then. "Well no, but okay let's sort this. No plucking lots of fucking and why not now?"

Vicky groaned. Was that potty mouth really her? She, who was so bloody closed mouthed she never even told her last partner she dared to go bare and did 'it' in the dark, was bandying words with a drop dead gorgeous guy from her … her what? She might have thought it was her past but was it? Really? And with hindsight her reticence was so unusual she should have known Maurice—what a wussy name—was not her taste. Actually she had, but chose to ignore it. The guy tucked his shirt into his underpants for goodness sake and Superman he wasn't. Now, her husband, for instance? By god he was a different matter entirely. Good grief, her pussy dripped, she salivated and her libido shouted *mine now, hurry up and fuck me.*

Oh lord, how times had changed.

"Look, if we're…" She paused, unsure how to express herself forcefully enough without cussing to high heaven. "Intimate," she said finally and cringed as his eyebrows disappeared under his hair line and he chuckled. Vicky punched his arm. "Oh you. You know what I mean. If we have that, then maybe I need a wee wakeup call?"

"Wee? You've been associated with the heathens from up north too much." He flicked her nose with his pinkie. "Oh no, my heart. Nothing short is allowed. Long drawn out sweet stings and tingles, rediscovering each other and learning how we mesh." He kissed the spot he had flicked. "Deep kisses that touch the soul, tiny touches, that sear the skin and leave a lingering mark of ownership. A tongue on the cunt, a hand on the cock, and finally, a hard pego ready to slip into a deep welcoming honeypot." He stroked her cheek and let his hand slide lower to stroke the circle of her neck, the swell of her breast and finally to encircled her nipple and pinch the hard nub one, then twice with enough force to make her gasp wince and sigh.

"Oh. More." Her pussy clenched as she imagined …what next.

"Onto the bed, my heart. Welcome me. Show me you want my touch." Kit spun her round, smacked her arse with enough force to make her stagger, and laughed as she squawked in surprise. "Now, get yourself ready and let's consummate the next phase of our journey together."

Vicky didn't think she'd ever moved so fast in her life.

With one hand she shoved condoms, tampons et al onto the floor, and with the other smoothed out the creases in the sheet so she didn't get crease lines on her butt. The only marks she wanted there were Kit's. Vicky wriggled and smiled.

"Yes, My Lord."

Kit's heart missed a beat and his breath hitched as he looked at her less than submissive demeanor. If only she meant it in every way possible. Even so, he chuckled as he followed her down with alacrity and pushed her to stretch out on her back, arms above head and legs apart with his knees wedged in between them.

His cock grazed her navel and she giggled. "Mr. Impatient there."

"Oh yes." With little or no finesse he nudged the entrance to her channel with the tip of his cock. If he had been of a fanciful bent he would have said her body unfurled for him like a flower in first bud. As he thought of himself as straightforward and without frills or furbelows, Kit discarded the thought as soon as it formed, waited a scant second, and thrust forcefully into her.

Victoria gasped, moaned and shook her head from side to side. "Oh yes, more now."

He'd never understand women, Kit thought as he set up a steady thrust and release that she followed smoothly, impeccably, beautifully, as her body tightened and loosed as required to give them most pleasure. Why the need to simulate rejection when all the while begging for togetherness and completion?

Too conscious of himself buried deep inside her, of her muscles tightening and contracting around him, Kit had no time to think of anything, other than he was where he wanted to be. He pinched each rosy nipple in turn and was rewarded by his wife's sweet mewls, and a new sheen of perspiration over her already sweat slicked shoulders.

She began to pant and Kit renewed his efforts. He wanted—needed—to fill her at the same time as he made her fly. To tumble into the abyss with her, to shout his completion and hear his voice mesh with hers just as their bodies did likewise.

Victoria shook and dimly in the recesses of his mind, Kit registered that telltale sign, let his iron will fall, and his senses take over. His seed gathered and with a roar he let it go to fill her.

She screamed and stiffened. Clutched his back so tightly he'd swear she drew blood, arched up towards him, and shuddered her own release around him.

It was a long time before he found the energy to move.

Eventually Victoria sighed. "You're squashing me."

Kit opened one eye and gazed down at her flushed face. "Pity. You make the perfect mattress." She giggled and punched his shoulder.

As a blow it was about as effective as a butterfly landing on your hand. As a mean of separating their bodies it worked perfectly. Her giggle combined with his mock jump and 'ouch' meant his pego slipped out of her with a gentle plop.

Kit rolled to one side, pinched her nipples in turn, kissed her cheek, and nose, and then let his lips linger on her mouth, before he rolled off the bed, stood up and stretched.

She watched him closely and did something strange with her thumb. He titled his head in question.

****

"A thumbs up. It means I like and appreciate what I see," Vicky said. "Like a Greek god."

He blanched. "Our God forbid. They have miniscule pegos and over inflated egos from what I can judge."

Hmm, maybe not the best comparison. "Like everything I desire?" she suggested instead. "All I ever want or need is you. My husband."

"Much better, dear heart." Kit bowed. "'Tis just as well. Now I'm about to play lady's maid as the servants have the night off to go to the ball. I'll fill your bath for you. The water should still be warm. Meanwhile," he gestured toward the elegant writing desk near one long window. "I noticed you'd filled your last journal, so I thought you might like a new one."

Vicky kicked off the tiny portion of sheet that still covered her feet and ankles and scrambled off the bed and across the room, heedless of her naked state. It felt so comfortable to be undressed she knew without a shadow of a doubt that when they were together it was the norm.

Also she understood that she unreservedly accepted she was his. Whatever happened, she should be with him.

The whys and wherefores she'd ponder over later.

As she pulled out the velvet covered chair and sat down at the desk, Kit laughed. "I'll shout you when the bath is ready."

"What? Oh yes, right thank you. Oh Kit." She lifted the leather bound book up reverently and stroked the soft hide cover. "This is beautiful. Perfect."

"My pleasure to please you, *ma petite*." He disappeared and she heard him whistle cheerfully over the sound of buckets of water being poured into the overlarge and ornate bath she'd glimpsed earlier.

Then water, whistling and men forgotten, Vicky returned her attention to the book in her hands. Slowly she rested it on the surface of the bureau, opened the cover and careful not to crease it, pushed it back to leave the first page ready to write upon.

With an almost childish glee, she found her quill, dipped it into her inkpot and set the sharpened quill end to the pristine page.

Victoria... Victoria who? Vicky realized she had no idea what her title was now. She shrugged and added, *Hopewell.* Kit could tell her otherwise after if need be.

December 1815

Dear diary,

Today has been a day full of surprises, not the least to discover that... Vicky lifted the quill, mindful she didn't want blots on the vellum. How could she explain all that had happened and not sound as if she needed committing to Bedlam?

She sniggered to herself. She'd be long gone before anyone read it anyway, so what did it matter? She bent to her task and continued to write until an itch on her spine made her lift her head.

Kit sat in a nearby armchair, with his robe loose around his shoulders.

She blinked and wiped her eyes. "Have you been there long?"

"Not too long. Come." He stood and held his hand to towards her. "The water is cooling."

Vicky nodded. "I've done enough for now." She pushed her seat back and took his hand to let him draw her onto her feet and rest against his chest. The silk of his robe whispered a caress over her shoulders as he shifted to hold her close.

"Kit, My Lord?"

He looked at her in enquiry as he stroked her hair in soothing rhythmic movements. "My Heart?"

"I do love you," Vicky strove to reassure him, and was rewarded by the loving smile that spread across his face. "I can see that you love me and I understand, and rejoice in the knowledge that, deep down you're mine. Only you and—" A large clap of thunder rent the air.

Vicky screamed. Behind Kit a door she hadn't noticed before stood open with a bright white light shining through it and created a pathway toward her. It gleamed and beckoned to her. Somewhere she heard a voice, hers? His? She had no idea

"Go or stay, only you can decide."

Go or stay where? How? Vicky took a step away from Kit. His face was expressionless, a blank canvas where so recently animation showed. His eyes were dark and shadowed. Unfathomable. Then she saw the agony there.

Go or stay... go or stay... go or ...

Another deeper clap of thunder shook the window panes.

BARE ALLEY INK: VOLUME ONE

Go...stay...
"Victoria."
"Vicky."
"Mama..."
Mama?

Chapter Eight

Faversham House, December 2015

Clara gasped behind him, and seemingly having thought better of her pretense of hiding, appeared next to him. Shifting nervously from foot to foot, she fidgeted with the hem of his shirt, which, now that she was standing, fell to mid-thigh. With her arms clasped around her middle, trying to hold the gapping ends together she looked uncomfortable, as confirmed by her next words.

"Don't say it, James. I'm not explaining why I'm half dressed, and wipe that smirk off your face. If you want to be helpful, run to my rooms and find me something decent to wear."

She shrieked when Daniel pulled her into his side. He needed the contact right now, because he knew that life as he knew it would change forever the minute he broke the seal on that envelope.

"I wouldn't dream of it, my lady. Besides, there is nothing wrong with being in a state of undress in the bed chamber of your affianced."

Clara gave a strangled cough, and Daniel found himself on the receiving end of the full imposing glare only the butler of a great house could give while maintaining a perfectly polite smile on his face. He had been the recipient of a similar glare from James's predecessor far too many times to count, when he'd come home after one of his youthful escapades.

Before he could say anything, Clara pulled away from him. He instantly missed her soft curves pressed into his side, and had to resist the urge to yank her back into his arms. The way her whole frame was quivering in seeming outrage, she'd probably kick him in the ballocks if he tried that.

"Stop this godforsaken Regency crap already. This is just us, and I know full well, you never approved of me taking over as curator, even though I'm damn good at my job. I'm not affianced to anyone, let alone Daniel, I—"

She stopped talking when James interrupted her by holding up his hand. The older man shook his head, and glanced toward Daniel as though he was looking for confirmation.

"You might not have been affianced, but you've been caught in a compromising situation with the Duke of Hockwell, and as is befitting his station, he will of course marry you to save your reputation." Again that sharp look at Daniel, which made him feel about five and meant he nodded his agreement. Strangely enough the thought of marriage didn't fill him with his usual dread. Quite the opposite. To be married to Clara, to have the right to explore her luscious body, and to know that no other man would ever touch what was his, felt right in a way that nothing had for as long as he could remember.

"Don't be ridiculous. This is 2015, not 1815, and there is no need to marry anybody. Jeez, will you tell him, Daniel?" Clara whirled round to address Daniel, and paled when he shook his head.

"You're not agreeing with him, surely? That's just…"

"Imperative," James said.

"Logical," Daniel said, and James inclined his head as they spoke those words in unison.

"You two … you cannot be serious. Who marries someone for those reasons? I sure as hell won't."

She was infuriating and adorable in equal measures, as she blew her hair off of her flushed face and stomped her foot for good measure. He would have such fun stamping out this behavior. Then again, it would be all kinds of amusement to encourage that bold side of her, because it would give him ample opportunity to think of punishing his duchess.

His cock jerked at those thought processes, almost as much as Clara's head as she looked between James and him.

"You will, my lady, because it is imperative that the Duke marries and provides an heir, according to the will of Lord Reginald Danvers."

"Well, bugger that." Clara's outburst made Daniel's lips twitch. She was clearly swearing even though he didn't understand the term. James in the meantime drew himself up to his full height.

"As to that, it is really not my kink, but who am to say what you and Duke Hockwell desire to get up to in the privacy of your bedchamber. In any case I shall retire, to leave you to settle this one way or the other."

James bowed to Daniel again, and ignored Clara's outraged spluttering.

"Unless my lord requires me for anything else, of course?"

Daniel shook his head, all too aware of the quietly seething woman in front of him.

"Well it's not all right with me. And what about the ball and—"

"The guests left when the electricity went down, my lady. I am shutting up the house and taking to my bed. I will be back in the morning with refreshments, and his lordship should be aware that the estate solicitor has been alerted of your presence. He will be making a special visit to talk about the practicalities of the duke's return."

James bowed again, but before he could turn to leave, Clara grasped the man's arm and stopped him.

"What on earth are you on about? Everyone cannot have just left. What about Vicky?"

There she went again with this Vicky person.

"Her ladyship is very well I'm sure. No, let me rephrase that, I am sure she has led a long and healthy life."

Clara looked all ready to hit him, and the fine hair on his neck rose, as a suspicion dawned on him. Surely not, but then again, he was here, and Kit's wife was...

"What the hell does that mean? Where is Vicky?"

James shot Daniel a look, and extricated himself out of Clara's clutches.

"Perhaps you would like to check the gallery."

He had barely finished that sentence before Clara shot out of the open door. Rumbles of thunder rolled through the air again, only serving to increase the itch between his shoulder blades. Her screech made his mind up for him, and when he rounded the corner, it was to see her standing in front of the portrait of Kit and his wife.

She traced the contours of Victoria, Duchess of Aulban's face, while whispering the same word over and over.

"Vicky."

*****

Through tears blurring her vision, Clara traced the contours of Vicky's face, and this Regency Duchess definitely was her Vicky. She would recognize the twinkle in the lady's eyes everywhere. Vicky and she might only have known each other a short time, but she'd truly felt as though she'd found the sister she never had. And it suddenly dawned on her she would never see her friend again.

The woodsy scent of the Duke of Hockwell's cologne—*oh god he really is the freaking duke*— alerted her to his presence seconds before a set of strong male arms wrapped around her waist, and pulled her back against his hard frame. His hot breath ghosted across her neck, as he nuzzled into her neck.

"Please don't cry, dearest." The unexpected endearment brought more tears to her eyes. God, why did he have to be sweet and concerned now? It made it almost impossible to resist him, and when he gently turned her, and lifted her chin up to study her face, Clara swallowed hard at the stormy emotions which crossed his features. One single muscle spasmed in his clenched jaw, and she couldn't tear her gaze away from that tic. It made her want to lean in and lick that part of his face, which was a completely inappropriate thought under the circumstances. As though he read her thoughts, and no doubt they were written all over her face, he ran his hand slowly down her back, until he could grasp one of her bare ass cheeks, and yanked her closer. His cock twitched between them and even through the fabric covering his shaft she could feel it branding her belly. A gasp escaped her lips, and a grim smile kicked up Daniel's lips, before he looked up at the painting of the wall, and his lips firmed into a thin line.

"Kit's wife is your Vicky, isn't she?"

"Yes." Clara somehow managed to get that one word out, and fought more of the blasted tears determined to fall down her face. A shiver went through her when he leant down and kissed the moisture left from her earlier outburst away. Her eyes fluttered closed of their own accord, and she pressed closer into him.

"I'm never going to see her again, am I?"

Their breaths mingled and she willed him to kiss her, to take away the emotions churning up her insides and to replace them with sensation. She needed to feel alive, to confirm that she wasn't dreaming, and that this strange warped reality was really her life from now on in.

Instead of claiming her lips, however, she felt him withdraw with sigh of regret.

"I think we really need to open that letter Aulban left for me."

Clara wrenched her eyes open to find him look at that letter as though he was expecting it to turn into poisonous snake.

"We do?" Her voice came out as a wobbly squeak.

Much to her surprise his harsh features broke into an affectionate smile. *Oh, god, that smile.* It made her nipples tingle, her breast heavy, and it meant she clamped her thighs together to stop the rush of hot need from trickling down the inside of her legs. Really, though, that smile ought to be registered as a deadly weapon of female pussy destruction. The dratted man clearly knew the effect he had on women too, because his piercing blue eyes crinkled up that the corners, and his eyebrow quirked in a decidedly naughty wink, before he sobered.

"Yes, my dear, I want you to read this with me, because this affects both of us. Besides, as my future wife and duchess you will need to know all the family secrets." He laughed at her outraged gasp, and without waiting for her reaction strode off back toward the bedchamber.

Clara followed at a more sedate pace, to stop herself from exploding at the return of the highhanded duke. His future duchess indeed. Over her dead body.

Some of her ire deflated, seeing him sat on the bed, turning the letter over and over in his large hands. Right now he didn't look very haughty, more like a little boy lost, and Clara's heart missed a few beats. He looked up when she approached, flung the letter on top of the bed, and twisted the signet ring on his pinkie.

"I can't. You open it and read it to me."

When she shook her head in surprise, he rubbed a hand over his face, and Clara could have sworn he was blinking away tears.

"*Please,* read it me."

It was the *please* that did her in. Not even bothering to make sure she didn't flash her bits and bobs at him in the process, she climbed up onto the high bed next to him, and after a glance at his tight set features, broke the seal.

A secret thrill went through her at the thought she held a piece of actual history in her fingers. While she was no stranger to holding artefacts from the past, it was always in controlled conditions with her hands covered in fine gloves to make sure she didn't damage the piece she was examining.

There was no finesse now, as she opened the heavy paper to reveal the elegant handwriting. Daniel inhaled sharply next to her, and rested his head on her shoulder, as she began to read.

July 1818 Aulban House, Derbyshire
Dear cousin,

I must admit I am feeling somewhat of a fool writing this letter and entrusting that it will reach you in the unspecified future, but I have great tidings. My dearest wife Victoria was safely delivered of twins this morning.

"Well, I'll be damned." Daniel's shout of surprise echoed her own squeak of wonder. He nudged her shoulder and his grin as she looked at him was infectious. "Two at once. What a good idea, shall we follow suit?" It made his azure eyes sparkle with mischief, and Clara's own lips twitched. He was much too … too everything for his own good.

"In your dreams mate, not mine."

"If you say so," he replied equably. "Go on, read on." Clara rolled her eyes and continued.

Barnaby and Sophia have a good pair of lungs, and I can already tell that Sophia will be a heart breaker. Victoria urges me to reassure you and Clara that she is well and happy. She seems to think that you will have been leg shackled by the voluptuous brunette I saw you with last. Personally I find this hard to believe.

Clara stopped reading and glared at the letter.

"Why would that be hard to believe? Am I not good enough for a duke, is that it? Insufferable man, how does Vicky put up with that?" Heat stained her cheeks when Daniel laughed, and she glanced up at him. The most curious expression flashed over his face, before he smirked.

"And I'm not freaking marrying you, no way, siree. I don't bloody know you."

That sculpted eyebrow of his rose again, and damn her traitorous hormones 'cause that move was sexy as hell.

"The correct address is still my lord, chit. And you will marry me, of that there can be no doubt, because if I am going to be stuck in this..." He glanced around the room, and grimaced toward the wet room. "This strange century and its new fandangled inventions, then I'm going to damn well hold onto the one person who makes me feel sane."

He grinned when her mouth fell open in surprise, and before she could guess at his intentions he swooped in and kissed her. All thoughts fled her brain as he traced the contours of her mouth with the tip of his tongue, silently urging her to submit to him. The letter fell out of her hands, and she grasped his shoulders for support, as he deepened the kiss, while tipping her backward onto the soft covers. Clara returned his kiss, hesitantly at first and then with bolder strokes of her tongue, until they were dueling with each other. By the time he wrenched his lips off of her his groan matched her sigh of surrender. His cock was a hard ridge against her thigh, and the bed dipped as he pulled away from her. Giving the letter no more than a cursory glance he strode off and using the boot jack at the far corner of the room, used it to yank off his Hessians. His breeches and stockings followed, until he stood there in his magnificent naked state. One large hand wrapped around his engorged cock, he fisted his shaft slowly, and Clara's mouth went dry when she saw the drop of pre-cum glisten at the tip of his shaft.

She opened her mouth to say something, anything, but no sound came out, just her harsh breathing. Clara couldn't tear her gaze from his cock. The man looked huge, heavily veined, thick and long, and she clenched her thighs to relieve the instant ache in her pussy.

While Clara had never actually had sex, she was no stranger to self-pleasure, and had used a variety of vibrators on herself. None of them had been as big as Daniel's cock, however, and shiver of apprehension marched up her spine.

"You have no idea how hard it makes me to see you looking at me like that, chit."

Clara wrenched her gaze slowly up his body, over the dips and valleys of abdominal muscles that would have put any twenty first century cover model to shame, the well-defined pectorals, broad shoulders, and strong neck, until finally she took in his clenched jaw and the burning need in his blue eyes.

It reflected the building heat in her lower belly so perfectly, she had to remind herself to keep on breathing, as her earlier arousal spiked once more.

"Daniel, I…" She couldn't continue, not when he advanced on her with the long limbed gait of a predator seemingly intent on devouring her. Lord help her, she was ready to be ravished any which way he wanted. The barely functioning rational side of her brain urged her to protest, while the submissive side demanded she melt. However, she managed a feeble objection as he climbed on the top, and slowly slid his big body over hers.

"What about the letter. Shouldn't we finish reading it, to find out what—"

The rest of whatever she was going to say was lost in the kiss he gave her. This wasn't a gentle kiss, far from it. This was a claim, a brand of her body and soul, as he took charge, reducing her to nothing more than a quivering mass of needing to be fucked now woman.

Sod the consequences. This heat building between them, the growing ache between her thighs was all that mattered, and when he finally broke the kiss and sitting up straddled her legs, and smiled at her, Clara was lost.

"If you don't want this, tell me now. Once I worked this darn shirt, which is spoiling my view of your luscious body off of you, I'm going to fuck you and make you mine."

****

The force of his feelings surprised Daniel. Even to his own ears his voice sounded hoarse, strained with need, and his cock would explode soon, he was sure. He hissed through his teeth when Clara ran her fingernails slowly down his body and then wrapped both her hands around his aching prick.

"I'm still not marrying you, *My Lord.*"

The intonation she put on his title made him shake his head, but as she chose that moment to pull back his foreskin and swipe her finger through the tiny slit of his cock head, he lost the ability to utter anything more intelligible than a grunt.

An impish smile kicked up her lips at his response and she lost her rhythm when he took the hem of his shirt and slowly lifting it, exposed her body to his view.

He dropped a kiss on each one of her nipples, breathing in her scent. When he flicked his tongue over one engorged bud, her moan in answer was music to his ears. Her fingers tightened on his prick, eliciting a grunt from him, and she hastily removed them.

"Sorry, did I hurt you?"

His Clara looked so worried, his chest tightened with emotion. He might only just have met her, but already she meant far too much to him, and regardless of her protestations to the contrary he would marry her.

"Yes, but you will soon ease that hurt. I want you, dear Clara."

Her eyes widened and the most delightful blush spread across her impressive bosom. Tugging at the shirt, he pulled it over her head. She arched her back to enable him to do so. The action meant her breasts touched his chest, and Daniel grasped the perfect globes and pushed them together, flicking his tongue over both her nipples at the same time.

Clara's breathing sped up and she pushed herself further into his mouth as he started to suck strongly.

"Oh god, that feels so good. Please…"

Daniel released the nipple between his teeth, scraping along the engorged bud, and grinned at the goose flesh that peppered his girl's skin. Her thighs bunched underneath him, and lifting off her, he nudged her legs apart with his thigh. The fact that she opened up willingly meant a great deal right now. It placed the head of his cock dangerously close to her wet cunt and they both groaned when he ran the tip of his prick through her cunt lips.

The urge to push into the sweet haven to be found between her legs rode him hard, but mindful of her innocence he teased them both by grasping the root of his shaft, and running it through her wet slit. More of her juices gushed out of her as she writhed underneath him, coating them both, as he bumped into her hidden pearl just visible at the top of her hood.

"Please, I'm so close, please, oh God, yes."

Her hips jerked upward and her little hole clenched, her inner lips darkening in color as the whole area swelled with the influx of blood as her arousal built.

Daniel allowed himself one last slow drag through her cunt, before he withdrew.

"How close are you, sweet girl?" he asked, and Clara groaned. Eyes closed with her glorious hair spread across his bed like a dark halo she looked a woman on the edge, caught up in her pleasure, and his prick twitched.

It would be so easy to sink his cock into her, but he needed to hear her say it. To know that she was his, and would not regret giving him her virginity in the morning.

"So, close, please, just do something."

Daniel grinned and scooting down the bed grasped her arse cheeks and lifted her cunt up to his face. He blew across the pink flesh in front of him, and Clare grasped the bed covers in a white knuckled grip. A keening cry escaped her as he licked along her slit, and he groaned his approval when her sweet nectar exploded on his taste buds. Was anything more delicious?

"Delicious, sweet, girl, and so very wet for me. Tell me this bounty is all mine to do with as I please. Tell me you're mine and want me to fuck you."

Clara clamped her thighs around his head, and her hips jumped under his hands, as she ground her cunt against his face.

"Yes, god, please…I'm so close…yes, yes…" The rest of her shout of completion came out as unintelligible jumble as sweet Clara came apart under his tongue. Daniel lapped up her juices, and kept up the gentle suckling on her hard nubbin until he'd wrung the last aftershock out of his girl, and her thighs grew slack. Only then did he lift his head and look up at her to see her watching him.

With her eyes at half-mast and her breasts still shaking with the force of her harsh breathing she looked sated and so beautiful it took his breath away.

"Hello there, my lady."

A giggle escaped her and her eyes grew wide when he slowly crawled up her body, delivering little kisses along her perspiration soaked skin as he went along. By the time he reached her face and claimed her kiss-swollen lips, she was squirming again underneath him.

"I enjoyed seeing you fall apart, my love," he said.

Clara gasped and began a tentative exploration of his torso until she reached the root of his cock. That organ jumped and a hiss escaped his lips, when she wrapped her little fist around it again.

"What about you, My Lord? Do you want me to—?"

"No."

Clara jumped at the terse command that came out much harsher than he'd meant it to, but he was hanging on by a thin thread here.

To make up for his brutishness he kissed her nose and smiled at her.

"While the thought of you taking my cock in your mouth is very appealing and we will definitely be doing this later on, I want to feel your internal walls quiver around my prick, while you take my seed, and lord help me, I want to spill inside your body."

Clara drew in a sharp breath and he hurried on to explain before she could voice an objection.

"However, I shall, of course withdraw and spill outside of your body, until we are married. It wouldn't do to—"

Her slap against his chest packed as surprising punch and he blanched as she let go of his cock and squeezed his ballocks in a grip so tight it brought tears to his eyes.

"I'm not going to marry you. I already said that, you fool of a duke. When I marry it will be because I'm madly in love with my groom, not because this sex on legs gorgeous time traveller took my virginity, and thus feels he *has* to marry me."

She mock glared at him, and dropped a kiss on his lips.

"Shush, you, let me speak," she continued in a tone that could strip paint. "This is the twenty first century, and we don't have to get married at all, unless we both want to. Regardless of what any old will might say. What we do need to do, however, is fuck. So will you please do that?" She paused and he wondered at her blush.

"There is no need for you to pull out. I've been on the pill since I was fourteen to regulate my cycle, so I can't get pregnant, and I suppose we ought to use condoms, but I dare say you have no idea what those are."

"You are talking in riddles, woman. Why can you not have children? And what in the deuce are condoms?"

Clara giggled, and he had to smile along with her. It was such a lighthearted sound it chased away the last of his misgivings, and she shrieked when he pushed her back on the bed and settled himself between her legs. A moan escaped her, when he teased her entrance with the head of his cock, and gritting his teeth, he pushed in just enough to feel her clamping down on his prick.

"Relax, sweet girl. Let me in. This might hurt at first, but it will be short lived pain, I promise."

"I know." Clara's breathless reply meant he pushed in a little bit more.

"God, you're so tight. I will not last long, I'm afraid. Are you ready?"

"Yes, god, yes, I …ow."

Catching her cry of pain in his mouth Daniel pushed through the thin barrier of her innocence in one swift move. After that first brief moment of resistance her sweet cunt opened to him beautifully. He stopped when he was fully seated inside her body, her internal walls quivering around his prick, and looked down on her. Eyes shut tight, his girl whimpered as she began to move slowly.

"Talk to me, my dear."

Her eyes fluttered open, and she gasped when he pulled almost all the way out, and then slid back into her.

"Talk? You expect me to talk?"

He laughed at the face she pulled.

"Not funny, just for the love of god, move….I… god yes… again….harder."

Daniel obliged, loving the incomprehensible sounds that spilled from Clara's lips, as he upped his pace. Her hips rose and fell in tune with his, as they established a rhythm and the heat built between them. Just like he feared his release built at the bottom of his spine far too soon for his liking, and slipping a hand between their sweat slicked bodies, he found her pearl and rubbed in tune with the ever increasing force of his thrusts.

Clara clamped around his cock and as the first pulses of his seed ejected, she too reached her pinnacle once more. Closing his eyes, Daniel gave himself up to the sheer joy of his release, as his future duchess shivered and shook underneath him, her little sounds of joy the perfect backdrop to his own guttural shout of completion as he made her his forever.

Daniel collapsed on top of her, and once their breathing had slowed down somewhat, and he was fairly certain that he had regained the use of his arms and legs, he withdrew his softening cock from the tight clasp her body still had on him. He clucked his tongue at her wince of pain, as he rolled off her, taking her with him and tucking her into his side. Clara snuggled into him with a sigh of completion and his heart clenched at her whispered words.

"Thank you."

Propping himself up on one elbow better to see her expression, he frowned down on her.

"What for, my precious girl?"

"For making my first time so spectacular," she said and he laughed.

"That is very sweet of you to say, dearest, but I fear I didn't last much longer than a school boy after he's graduated to long trousers. I can do much better than this. Just give me a few moments to recover, and I'll show you."

Clara smiled and much to his surprise raised herself up until she could kiss him. Just like before their kiss quickly turned passionate, and his cock responded most satisfactorily. Clara gasped in seeming delight when he grasped her by the shoulders and held her poised above his erect cock.

"Your turn to ride me, if you're not too sore that is."

With an adorable look of concentration on her face, Clara grasped the root of his cock and slowly seated herself. Her breathing sped up in tune with his, and grasping his shoulders to steady herself, began a slow up and down rise, that made him grit his teeth against the urge to take over.

"That's it my sweet girl, you set the pace."

She grinned at him, and then her brows drew together in a frown as she looked past and to the side of him.

Following her gaze he saw it was the letter Kit has written to him.

"Shouldn't we finish reading that?" She gasped as he thrust his hips upward to meet her on the down stroke, and digging his finger into her hips, Daniel did it again.

"Plenty of time for that. Besides I know what it will say."

"You do?" Clara went a little cross eyed, and shrieked when he tumbled them both, as he took charge of their coupling.

"Yes, I do. He'll wish me well and laugh at my expense that I had to go through time and space to find the one woman I want to marry."

Clara tensed and shook her head.

"I told you, I'm not going to marry you. I want to marry for love and… umph."

Daniel shut the infuriating woman up by kissing her while speeding up his thrusting.

"Yes you will, even if it takes me the rest of your days to convince you of it."

Chapter Nine

Clara woke up on her own the next day. By herself in the big Regency four poster bed with bright sunshine streaming into the room, signaling that she must have slept half the day away. She could almost believe that she had dreamt last night's strange happenings. Were it not for the soreness between her legs and the feel of Daniel's cum slowly slipping out of her as she gingerly moved into an upright position, she might well have believed that to be true.

As it was she hugged her arms around herself and grinned as she recalled the events of last night in glorious Technicolor detail. It was a wonder she could walk at all this morning as she padded across to the wet room to relieve herself and freshen up a bit.

Her reflection in the mirror gave her pause for thought. She looked happy, truly happy and she was honest enough with herself to admit that was entirely due to her time travelling duke. Where was he, she wondered? Padding back into the bed chamber she picked up her mobile phone and whistled through her tears.

It was 2.00 PM in the afternoon, and James had said the estate solicitor would be around in the morning for the reading of the will. The whole thing was still a mystery to her. At some point in the early hours of the morning Daniel had read the rest of the letter to her. A fair part of it has been this Kit fellow ripping off Daniel, just as he'd said he would, and she smiled to herself as she recalled the affection in Daniel's voice when he'd talked of Kit and his wife.

It had reassured her greatly that by whatever

quirk of fate this whole thing had happened, Vicky… no Lady Victoria… was happy in her times. She could only hope that Daniel would be happy in this time.

A noise from the sitting room brought with it the scent of freshly brewed coffee, and mindful of the fact that it was probably James, she grasped a robe draped over the chair at the writing desk perched in front of the window, just in time to see the solicitor's Range Rover speed away up the winding drive that led to Haversham House.

Daniel would have had his meeting then and would now be installed as the Duke of Hockwell, long lost heir to the Haversham Estate, and by default her employer.

Good grief, I'm a walking cliché. I'm sleeping with the boss.

That's if he didn't sack her. Would he even have a need for a curator now, that he was the duke and in charge of the family fortune?

The thought that she might never see him again hurt far more than it ought to, and Clara shook her head against her fanciful thoughts. You just didn't fall in love with anyone that quickly, did you? That was the stuff of romance novels, that was all.

The door to the bed chamber opened, effectively cutting off her maudlin thoughts. Far from James it was Daniel carrying a tray with coffee, and what looked like brunch. It wasn't the incongruous sight of this Regency duke doing such a menial task, however, that took her breath away. No, that would be due to the sight of Daniel in modern day clothing. The faded designer jeans clung to his strong legs, and hugged the impressive bulge at his groin, which she was now intimately acquainted with. A light jumper, the sleeves pushed up to reveal his corded forearms, completed the ensemble and made her mouth water and her pussy clench.

One night of sex and I've turned into a nymphomaniac.

Daniel winked at her as he sat the tray down on the writing desk, dislodging a leather bound book that thudded onto the floor. He bent to pick it up with a frown and Clara's fingers itched to grasp the globes of his ass and squeeze them as the denim stretched over them.

Naturally he caught her staring when he turned around book in hand, and he smirked.

"As much as I'd like to take you up on that invitation, dear girl, you'll be too sore, and besides you need to eat something to keep your strength up first."

He laughed when she blushed, and handing her the book, dropped a hard kiss on her lips.

"That looks like one of the diaries Kit's wife was always scribbling in. No doubt it will put your mind at rest as to the whereabouts of your friend." He nodded at her sharp intake of breath, as she opened the leather bound volume to the first page.

She recognized Vicky's writing immediately.

December 1815

Dear diary,

Today has been a day full of surprises, not the least to discover that...

"Good, god, you're right, this is Vicky's writing and she seems to have started this the morning after she was abducted."

"Abducted, you say?" She looked up at the amusement she could hear in Daniel's voice. "Strong word that, abduction, and it mirrors the tone of the will, which was amusing to say the least. I do believe Lord Reginald Danvers might have been quite mad."

Daniel poured her a cup of coffee, handed her it, and taking the diary out of her hands, flicked through the pages with a whistle.

"This is a day by day account of their life together it seems. There must be more of these. I wonder where we would find them. I must ask my curator."

He grinned in his most mischievous way yet, when her sip of coffee went down the wrong way, and he leaned his jeans clad butt on the edge of the writing desk, seemingly waiting for her to recover.

"I am still the curator then?" She flinched when both his eyebrows rose, and he inclined his head. Right now, modern clothes or not he looked every inch the haughty Regency duke again, and her heart beat faster. How she loved that look on him. *Loved?*

No, no, no, I can't be in love with him.

"Of course you are. The estate solicitor was full of praise for the work you've done here." He frowned and inclined his head. "I owe you my heartfelt thanks for getting us out of the mess your predecessor left us in." He put his hand up to stop her immediate denial. Truly, though he hadn't been that bad, and the conditions imposed by the will, were bizarre to the extreme. "No. let me get this off my chest. I will take me weeks, if not months to sort through all the paperwork, and I can't think of anyone else I would trust to go through it all with me, and not pull the rug out from under my feet." He stopped to smile at her, and Clara's heart beat faster at the approval she read in his eyes.

"It's okay. That's my job, and I'm glad to see you've given up on this marrying me nonsense."

"Did I say that?" His voice held an edge of steel and made her pussy tingle. "As you keep telling me this is the twenty first century, and thus I can see no reason why my wife could not also hold down gainful employment."

Clara was glad she hadn't been drinking or she

would have spat her coffee out.

"I told you, I won't marry without—"

"Love, I know. Neither will I, and I will just have to convince you that I'm a man you can fall in love with then, won't I?"

Epilogue

Haversham House, three years later

Clara giggled as Daniel, the Duke of Hockwell, shouldered open the door to their bedroom, and with an exaggerated huff carried her across to the four-poster bed and collapsed with her on the modern memory foam mattress.

"Good lord, woman, what is in that dress of yours, stones?"

"Well, my lord, you did insist on a grand wedding with all the trimming and this family heirloom of a dress. It weighs a ton and I can't wait for you to peel me out of it." She smiled when Daniel kissed her nose, having had to push several yards of material out of the way to find that part of her.

"True, but it was my mother's dress and when we found it in the attic I knew I wanted you in it. Mama would have approved and you looked radiant."

"Flattery will get you nowhere." Clara gasped as her new husband somehow found his way under the multitude of petticoats that came with the dress and cupped her bare pussy with his hand. *Liar*. It would get him everywhere, not that she intended to divulge that nugget of information to him. Some things were best kept to yourself.

"I don't need to flatter my wife. You, sweet thing are all mine, now, and what a naughty duchess I've got. All wet for me already and no underwear. Mama would be outraged." He slid one long finger inside her, and Clara moaned as her body instantly responded to the man she loved.

"No she wouldn't. I know fine well that they didn't wear any undergarments in those days."

Daniel curled his finger upward while pressing his thumb to her clit, eliciting a low moan from Clara.

"No wonder my overachieving cousin ended up with seven kids."

Clara gasped and then pouted as Daniel withdrew his fingers and licked them clean with a devilish gleam in his eyes.

"I'm glad cousin Linda managed to attend anyway. You could definitely tell she was a descendant however many times removed from Kit and Victoria." He grinned and shrugged his shoulders. "We tried to work that out but gave up after goodness how many greats."

Clara swallowed hard and nodded her agreement when Daniel got off the bed and proceeded to shrug out of his wedding coat and tails, and opened the bottle of champagne that James had left to cool for them on the nightstand with great aplomb. Having filled a flute each with the bubbly liquid he handed her one, and they clinked glasses, grinning at each other like love sick fools, which was, of course, exactly what they were.

True to his word, Daniel had set on a course of determined seduction, following on the morning of what they now laughingly called *The Dukes' Abductions*.

Just like any good romance novel their abductions had ended up in a happy ever after for all concerned. Through the meticulously kept diaries they had eventually discovered, they'd learnt all about the lives of Vicky and Kit, and Clara knew, Daniel had appreciated knowing how his cousin's life had turned out as much as she had appreciated the knowledge that Vicky had been happy.

For his part Daniel had adapted to life in the

twenty first century with great ease. The fact that he hadn't been afraid to lean heavily on her for guidance had been a pleasant surprise and had meant that Clara had fallen in love with him even more.

So, last Christmas when he'd very formally had gone down on one knee in front of a crowded ball room, she had been only too happy to accept.

"Penny for your thoughts, at least I think that's the right expression. And I hope they are about me, or a man could get jealous seeing the love of his life smiling like that about someone else."

Clara grinned at the mock pout that accompanied those words, and she stuck her tongue out at him.

"Careful, there, girl. I got you to myself now and you don't want to start your honeymoon with your behind on fire." At her moan in reply he grinned. "Then again, maybe you do, and I shall be most happy to oblige. I have a new flogger with your name on it, girl."

"Is that supposed to be deterrent, *my lord*?" Clara fluttered her eyelashes at him and Daniel burst out laughing.

"Minx, just as well I love you."

Clara sobered, and a thrill of excitement went through her at his husky words.

"As I love you, my duke."

The End

www.dorisoconnor.com

www.ravenmcallan.com

EVERNIGHT PUBLISHING ®

www.evernightpublishing.com